BEYOND BEDROCK

THE BEDROCK SERIES | BOOK THREE

BRITNEY KING

WWW.BRITNEYKING.COM

ALSO BY BRITNEY KING

BEYOND BEDROCK

BRITNEY KING

COPYRIGHT

Hot Banana Press

Front Cover Design by Lisa Wilson

Back Cover Design by Britney King

Cover Image by Sebastian Kullas

Copy Editing by TW Manuscript Services

Proofread by Proofreading by the Page

First Edition: 2015

ISBN: 978-0-9892184-9-8 (Paperback)

ISBN: 978-0-9892184-3-6 (All E-Books)

britneyking.com

To the crazies.
For without the experience of
dealing with you—
this story could not have been written.

PROLOGUE

It was rocky right from the start. Right from the get-go, I guess you could say. From the day I saw him on the street. But you have to hang in there. Really, it gets better. It was quite by accident, our chance encounter that day. I mean, sure, of course I'd been watching him. But I hadn't intended for us to come face to face, not like that. He was walking with his stepson, with *her son* in the city. They'd come from his office and I wasn't sure where they were headed, to lunch I assumed, but then that was partly why I kept following. I had to know.

I was several steps behind them, I knew to keep my distance. Even then. *Especially* then. It wasn't that I didn't want to be close to him. I did. But more than that, I wanted to *see* without being *seen*. That's when it happened. The kid had been holding something in his hand and he dropped it. I watched it fall. William was looking off, somewhere down the street. Who knows. That's why he didn't see the boy stop or notice the car making a right on red, not the way I did. The car rounded the corner, quickly, *too* quickly. The driver clearly wasn't paying attention. He didn't see the boy crouched down. Not the way I did. I hadn't wanted to be seen, of course, I hadn't. Instinct took over. I threw myself into the front end of the vehicle, palms out. My mouth formed the word STOP but I don't think anything came out. It was too late. The kid was on his feet, safe, out of the way and I was on my back with the love of my life standing over me. That much in and of itself made everything else all right.

"Are you ok?" he asked. I could see that he was visibly shaken. I remember that he'd checked the kid to make sure he was in one piece before he turned his attention to me. I told him I was fine and then he paced a little. I could see that he was thinking of what might have been, although not too much about it. For the most part, he was calm, in control, careful not to let the mask slip. I think he was thinking about me, about what to do with the woman laying on the pavement, grateful that she ended up with nothing more than a few minor scratches and some bruising. I wondered if it had been worse, whether he'd have felt remorseful for not being more precautious. Looking back, I can't say for sure. Even now, I don't know if he remembers. Does he know it was me? Or was it all very random to him?

"You should have been watching," I managed to say and he nodded.

"Thank you," he said and then he was gone, his security guys stepping in between, ushering him on.

It's too bad they hadn't been watching properly or certainly they would have seen. What good is it if they're only there to clean up the mess? That's the way most people are, I've found. They see what they want to see. They're looking for the bad guys, the big threats. The *real* danger. Not women who save little boys from getting crunched into a million pieces. They should be thankful they have me around, I recall thinking. *What they don't know won't kill them.* At least not today.

The therapist looked up from the paper, having read what Lydia had written. "This is a good start," she said.

Lydia nodded.

"So, this was your first memory of William Hartman?" she asked waving the paper in the air slightly. "Saving his child?" It's difficult to make out what she's saying given the pen shoved between her teeth but her exact words matter little. Lydia already knows where this is going.

"No," Lydia said.

"No?" she asked, cocking her head, narrowing her eyes. "But you said—"

"It wasn't his child," Lydia corrected. "It was *hers.*"

"I see."

Lydia pressed her lips together, her expression hopeful. "So, you'll give me my things back, then?"

The woman shakes her head. "Some of the items you requested your mother bring are against the rules Ms. Hammons. I'm afraid—"

"The pen and paper, specifically."

The paper she wants, the pen, well, she'll have to figure something else out considering said pen is currently wedged between the woman's teeth. It's vile and it's disgusting how a person with a higher ED degree can be so ignorant about germs, about other people's possessions. *Although, possession is nine-tenths of the law. Typical.* Unclinical. *This one should be a breeze.*

The woman considered her question for a moment before offering a response. "If you think it'll help, writing things down…"

Lydia shrugged. "Don't you?" she asked nodding toward the paper in the woman's lap.

"You make a fair point Ms. Hammons," she said. She

followed up with a fake smile. "We're going to get you a different pen. This one is against our safety regulations," she added, raising her brow. She removed the pen from her mouth and studied it closely. "Also, I quite like it."

"Consider it a gift," Lydia said. The woman smiled, this time it wasn't as fake and that's how Lydia knew they were getting somewhere.

❧

9:03 AM

Dearest William,

Schizoid personality disorder. This is the official diagnosis. It's amazing, really. Amazing that they think they can label a person using three words and BAM... that's who they are. Well, let me tell you. THEY are wrong. They think some scribble scrabble on a piece of paper gives them the right to tell me who and what I am. Ha. THEY ARE THE CRAZY ONES!

I am not those three words. Nope. I am a whole lot more than that. For one, I am a human being. And two, (trust me, this is where it gets good) I am in love with you. Deeply, madly, in love with you. What can I say? Love makes people do crazy things. Everyone knows that.

Just this morning, I picked out a light blue top and jeans to wear. For you. For this occasion. To match your eyes, but also because blue signifies loyalty and honesty, and this is why I write. Because I will show them, and I will show you. I am more than a label.

It wasn't easy at first. When I began writing to you in here, I mean. Honestly, I had no idea where this whole thing would take me. I simply picked up my pen, set it down, and thought of you—I thought about what I wanted to say and the best way to say it.

It's been several weeks now, and I can feel things winding down. I believe this chapter is coming to an end. And by the end, specifically, my time in this place.

8

BEYOND BEDROCK

This will likely be my final chapter to you and every writer knows it's important to go out with a bang. As for what comes after, I do not know.

Because that's the thing, my love. Something always comes after. Bangs don't just occur, people just don't go down, and that's the end of it, you know. Someone has to pay. That is a true ending. Revenge. Retribution. Complete and utter destruction. That's what love does, you see.

Alas, as I ponder how this part of our story will end, I realize endings are never truly endings and this brings me great comfort. That's why it's important to get this right. I know this deep down in my bones and so I carry on. I do the work. I balance the tray on my lap, consider my plan for a moment, and then place the notebook on top of it. I pause and consider how much to tell you, here and now, before we are finally together again, and so I simply stare out the window and think of your eyes.

As I watch the trees swaying in the wind, I think about the breeze and what it would feel like across my skin. If I had to guess, I'd say a lot like your lips. I feel like I'm forgetting the simple things. Things like the sound of leaves rustling, the warmth of the sun on my face, the smell of *real* food, not the slop they serve in here. Through the double-plated glass windows, I swear I can almost hear the birds chirping, and I think of you and the sound of your voice calling my name. It is then I realize I want my work and my time in here to have meant something. It has to.

It is also then that I truly understand the significance of her visits. This isn't just about her. It isn't about her getting the facts—*her* side of the story.
It is about *our* story. It's about the story of our love. And then it hit me....

Who better to tell that story than me? That's what this all means.

This was never about her at all.

It was about us.

You and me.

This is our story and it has been my love letter to you.

In the spirit of the colors I'm wearing, and since we're being honest here, I want you to know I have written this for you. I have told our story in hopes you might come to understand the depth and the expansiveness of my love for you. So, that by the time we are together again, in just a matter of hours now, you will see things differently.

I don't know how or why things got so mucked up, William. I don't. I only know that I am in here and you are out there. I know you have been confused about our feelings for one another. And I also realize this, our story, my work in progress, will fix it all.

Today, as I write this, I am unlike the birds I can so faintly make out chirping just beyond these bars. These walls. I am locked away on a 5150 involuntary psych hold, which was extended from seventy-two hours to fourteen days. Tomorrow there is to be a hearing.

But for the past thirteen days now, I've been trapped, in a cage, living as an animal, essentially—and likely, I understand, at your doing. Not because I've done anything wrong—but because you have friends in high places.

How could such a thing as sweet and pure as love be wrong, anyway, William?

Riddle me that.

But the good news is… it won't be long now.

They can't keep me locked in here forever.

Plus, I have a plan. I'm sure you of all people understand that. And William, my dear William, if there is anything you should know, know that I am not angry with you. There's not one ounce of bitterness in me toward you—only love. Always, only love. I want to be angry. Sure I do. But how could I be angry with someone whose love for me is so vast and so true that he has to keep me locked up just so he has me all to himself? It's like a fairy tale, really.

It was brilliant, honestly. And so very you, William. Just like the blue shirt I wear, you're loyal.

Not just to me, to your wife as well. I understand that now. Even if I don't necessarily like it... I understand.

You're sending me a message.

Because underneath all of that loyalty, like the shirt I wear, you're blue. The message you send is loud and clear—you want me as badly as I want you. I'm good at sensing these things. I always have been. But this doesn't mean it's easy, William. Being in here, your antics. *Her.* True love never is though, is it?

I do get upset from time to time and I do things. Bad things. *Necessary things.* Things I will tell you about someday soon— when we are together. It's just a matter of time as I help you to understand. In the meantime, before we can be together, skin on skin, flesh on flesh, I accomplish what I need to share in my writing. It's the only way now. I will trade her. My story—our story—will be my letters to you, and they will set the record straight. It will be like sending messages in a bottle and we will get it right.

Soon enough, though, I will be like the birds I hear in the distance, free from this cage. Free to express my love for you in all the ways that count.

Until then, it should bring us both great comfort to know, that in my mind, I am like the birds now—here, in this moment. I am free. Free from labels. Free to love who I want to love and to know he loves me in return. They can hold me here, physically, but they can never control my mind.

This story, the story of us, is proof. It is my song to you.

Kisses,

L

P.S. I wrote you a poem:

One can only deny the truth

for so long.

Forever, maybe.

But forever has nothing on

the way I feel about you.

~

CHAPTER ONE

Ten Days Prior

As she sat at her kitchen table with the notes laid out before her, she considered how today's meeting with Lydia had gone. Not terrible. But not great either. Probably about as well as one might have expected. All things considered.

God, she needed a drink. She'd kill for a drink. Given her current predicament, she realized that probably wasn't the best analogy. But still. Something to take the edge off would be nice. Sobriety seemed to be a double-edge sword in times like these. Knowing there was only one vice left these days she could rely on, she picked up the coffee she'd poured, placed her lips to the cup and stared out the window. The coffee, still too hot to drink, taunted her. She blew into the mug and then took a small sip, knowing it would burn her. *Just the way Lydia Hammons would. If she let her.* She understood she'd need to be careful, if she were going to proceed down this road. Lydia Hammons' therapist had gone so far as to warn her personally. She couldn't advise her specifically, but she could suggest the visits cease. And she had.

She sat that way for a while, mug pressed to her lips, not drinking, not doing much of anything. She was *thinking. Waiting. So much of their lives amounted to nothing more than waiting these days.*

Even still, she wasn't sure she could keep going. Maybe the therapist was right. Maybe it was pointless. It was certainly risky. To keep reading, to keep searching was putting herself in jeopardy. How much she didn't quite know. She only knew she had to keep going. She was tired. Hence the coffee in the middle of the day. Already, their meetings had taken a toll on her, given everything she'd been through. Now, the stakes were higher. There were lives at risk. If she weren't careful, trying to get to the bottom of this, trying to get this story just might kill her.

Eventually, she gave up on waiting for the fix she so desperately needed to cool, placed the mug back on the table and turned her attention back to the letter. Coffee, life, *everything* would have to wait.

As she turned the pages over in her hands, she let the words replay in her mind. She'd known Lydia to be crazy right from the start—that was no secret. But she hadn't exactly predicted she'd be so cunning. And definitely, not *this* clever.

She eyed the words on the page, sighed, and pushed the letter away. What was laid out before her was hard to read and even more difficult to make sense of. Still, if there were an answer to be found that would save the people she loved, a plan, *anything*—a rhyme or reason to it all, she would be the one to find it. *She had to.*

She was on a mission.

She would pull herself together.

She would fix this.

She would get inside the mind of Lydia Hammons.

Even if it killed her.

She was determined.

And so, she finished her coffee and she read.

The Story of Us.
By Lydia H.

I knew I loved him from the first moment I saw him. I wore black as sure and as dark as night. It wasn't like you'd think... He didn't smile and take my hand the way I imagined. Our coming together actually wasn't like that at all. It was an ordinary morning, early spring, the sun bright and yet still further away than one knew it soon would be. Soon the heat would be all consuming, soon it would sear your skin, burn your eyes. Our love would burn just the same. That's the funny thing about it all. Isn't it? Everything shifts eventually. *Everything.*

Speaking of love, it wasn't supposed to happen like this. I didn't believe in love at first sight, at least not *before*. I do now. I can still recall the moment it all changed. It's as though it happened just yesterday. I was brushing my teeth— half-listening to the morning news and half dreading going to the office. I hated the office. Mostly, I hated people. I brushed harder and watched the blood drip onto the porcelain as the crushing weight of the anxiety set in. I felt the familiar buzz; the low hum of noise that always precedes a full-blown panic attack. And then, all at once, I heard his voice and something inside me shook, something shifted in the world. This was what I'd been waiting for. *He was what I'd been waiting for.* The antidote to all life's conundrums. And when I heard that familiar voice, *I knew.* As he spoke, the buzzing stopped and there was clarity and crispness to the day, to my life, like I'd never known. At once, my vision for the future became focused and sharp.

Sure, I knew his name. Who wouldn't, given all that had happened? I'd even gone so far as to make plans for us to meet. I just hadn't acted on them yet. I'd avoided him and anything even closely resembling what had once been—just like I avoided germs and crowds full of people. Crowds of people are overwhelming, (not to mention germ-infested) they're intimidating, foreign, and unknowing.

And until that moment, so was William Hartman.

I spat the last of the blood into the sink and dropped the toothbrush onto the counter like the omen that it was. Then I turned my full attention back to the television where it belonged and wondered how it was possible anything on this earth could be so utterly perfect. I was aware I wasn't supposed to feel this way. Of course, I was. I knew I wasn't supposed to feel that sort of attraction. Given what he'd taken from me, that is. But there he stood, in his crisp white shirt, suit, and tie, the whole of him—filling up so much space. As he spoke, he touched his tie and in one single movement sucked the air right out of the room, and with it, the air from my lungs. It was astonishing. Such a tiny fluctuation on his part, given what I knew he was capable of. But suddenly he set everything right in my world, and I wondered, *why now?* He was speaking on the Gleason merger, I remember it all so clearly. He might as well have been speaking gibberish for all I cared, but I knew then we would become close. It was remarkable. It was meant to be. I didn't know when or how, but I knew I'd find a way. My father taught me that 'where there's a will, there's a way!'—

one of the few good things he'd ever imparted upon me—if we're being honest here, and we are.

I watched as he wrapped up the interview, so capable, so in control, and I no longer felt panicked or unease. I felt lighter and thinner.

Just like the black I wore.

Finally, I had a purpose.

And that purpose was meeting him.

~

HER MOOD WAS RED HOT LIKE THE SHIRT SHE WORE. ON THE day of their first visit, Lydia knew she was on fire. She was on a role. *She was playing a role.* She'd ace this thing. She smiled, considering how long it had been since they'd last seen one another. *Too long,* she thought, picking at a faded thread which hung from the borrowed shirt she wore. She smoothed the shirt across her sunken belly, reveling in what the day had in store for her. Lydia fingered the thread, smiled, and caught the end of it. She twirled and twisted it between her thumb and forefinger, watching as it unraveled —not unlike she herself had done. She pulled a little more marveling at the irony of it all. *That's how it happens.* One teensy snag and suddenly, a pull this way or that way, and it becomes a whole other matter altogether. It amused her a great deal that one simple analogy pretty much summed up the entirety of her life. But that was a story for another day.

For now, she'd decided she'd gained what she'd been after —finally. A visitor!

It wasn't polite to withhold information, she knew that.

But it was smart. That's why Lydia decided to wait her out. She studied the thread she'd wrapped around her pinky and pulled tighter until her finger went from pink to purple to a beautiful shade of blue. Still, she pulled tighter. *She always had liked that shade of blue.*

Somewhere far off, she heard an unknown tune hummed, and she attempted to match it with the whirl of the ceiling fan above. She turned her ear ever so slightly toward the music, but the one thing she didn't do was look at the woman adjacent to her. She didn't need to. It was enough she felt the woman's gaze burning into her skin. She could feel things, she could feel *everything* which made visuals unnecessary in times like these. *She was on fire.* She knew who the woman was and why she'd come and the rest was history.

Lydia cleared her throat and pulled tighter at the string. Later, she would come to realize that such a thing was her meal ticket. She had work to do, still, so she released the thread just a little and spoke slowly without looking at the woman directly. "I know why you're here," she said, losing at her own game. She waited for a response and when none came, she shrugged nonchalantly. "You want answers... I get it."

"I do want answers," the woman replied slowly.

Lydia raised her brow. She did meet her adversary's eye. "I'm only going to agree to tell you my side of the story, which is what you want, isn't it—if you agree to let me do the telling," she said, tilting her head.

"Why else would I be here?"

"You see," Lydia said. "That's the thing—I've worked it out already, and I've decided I'm going to go ahead and let you in —in order to share our story. His and mine, that is. But first, you should know, despite any preconceptions you might have, that this is about love. What I will share with you is the truth as I know it, and I won't allow you or anyone else to deny me that."

The woman glanced at her expensive, over-priced shoes and then looked up at Lydia.

Lydia smiled. "And if we are going to do this—and it seems we are, or you wouldn't be here, then we're either going to do it my way... or not at all."

"What does that mean to you?"

"It means that I will teach you the rules of the game, and you will listen. We will play together. Because only then will you understand, there are many sides to the truth. And no one wins a game of this kind. Not really."

The woman exhaled slowly. *Already, she was listening.* She narrowed her eyes. "What makes you think I want to play your games?"

Because you're here.

The woman pressed her lips to one another. "Haven't you considered that I've had enough? That maybe we all have..."

"You want the story. I know you do," Lydia told her, cocking her head. "Otherwise you wouldn't be here."

Lydia had expected a response. Instead she watched as the woman stood and walked to the door, opening it hesitantly. She turned and paused just inside the frame. "I want answers; you're right about that much, at least," she said looking back over her shoulder. She shook her head slightly. "But you see, it takes two people to play a game, Lydia. And only one of us here is playing."

Lydia offered the woman a smile even though both knew this was no smiling matter. Still, it was a pleasant smile. The kind that welcomed one in and invited them to stay awhile. Paradoxically, Lydia shook her head. "That's where you are wrong."

~

1:33 PM

Dear William,

Today marks my second day here and the first visit from her.

I have already decided that I will help her.

But she doesn't know that yet.

I will tell her what she wants to hear.

And likely a few things she doesn't.

I think that in order to truly help her—to help us all; I have to take it back to the beginning. When we were all happy.

I see a pattern evolving here. I think you can see it, too. This is my specialty—seeing patterns—finding similarities. It is one reason you have come to love me, as I know you do. But then, you already know this. It was my knack for seeing the possibility, even back then, on that very first day as I watched you on the news. I listened to your words ring aloud in my head, and from that, I understood the magnificence of timing and the reason it all played out just like magic.

Ironically, though, and sadly to her detriment, it would be your wife who loved me first. But if it is any consolation, I will tell you this—in a perfect world, my dreams sometimes still include Addison. There are days I picture us as one big happy family. Of course, you love me more (and will always) because your love for me is in direct proportion to my love for you. Unlike Addison, my feelings for you are so wide and so deep that few people, aside from the two of us, can grasp what exactly it is that means. Or the lengths we would go to for one another. Just like what you did by placing me in here. It's extreme, but that's us, William. Always has been, always will be.

Also, since I'm wearing blue like your eyes and well, because blue signifies honesty, I have to admit it's only on the good days that I imagine your wife being a part of our plan. Most days, I face the unfortunate reality of the situation (even more so now that I'm in here!). I know as long as she's in the picture, the more I realize she will only ever come between us. *Oh, how she likes to get in the way.*

Also, she makes you upset, William.

She provokes you and changes your mood. She sucks your energy away. She takes everything. She does the same to me. It's her fault the highs are so high and the lows are much too low.

Addison is black magic. She does things to people. I know... I've seen it firsthand.

It happened the first time I ever met her.

Which, as hard as it is to believe, was six months ago now.

I guess it is as they say, time flies when you're having fun.

And I like to think we are.

Kisses,

L

P.S. I wrote a poem for you. I hope you like it.

There are so many parts and pieces

to the both of us.

Just think—

Of what we might amount to

if we put them all together.

~

LYDIA SHOWED UP PREPARED FOR THEIR SECOND VISIT. SHE'D carefully prepped herself, choosing her attire wisely, managing her appearance to have the greatest effect. She understood how important these things were which is why she wore a green sweater— to match the plants she tended and to signify harmony. *Also growth.* That's what this visit was to be about. *Everything had a purpose.*

Lydia looked on as her opponent picked up the papers before her and studied them.

For now, they were enemies—but it wouldn't always be this way. Soon, there would be harmony between them as sure as the color green she wore. That was the goal. She wanted this. She wanted *her.* She wanted her to be on her side.

Lydia studied the intricacies of the hardened expression the woman wore as she read the words that had been carefully crafted just for her. Well, for William truthfully—but she couldn't—or rather *shouldn't* say as much now. Lydia noticed the way her opponent's nose curved a little, clearly broken once, a long time ago. She noted the way her eyebrows were meticulously over groomed. Maybe Lydia would do this to her own. *Like the color green one wore to blend in.* These were the little nuances she studied. Soon enough she would memorize them by heart. That's where she'd write them, tuck them away for safekeeping.

Understanding the art of war, Lydia spoke first. "We're going to write the story together."

The woman glanced up and drew a long breath. "Is that so?"

Lydia wasn't put off by her rudeness, by her lack of commitment to the cause. She understood the woman needed her more than she wanted to admit.

They always did.

Things may have looked grim on her side of the table from where the other woman sat, but Lydia knew better. Everything would work out just as it should.

She would pull herself together.

She would fix this.

She would make everything right again.

Even if it killed her.

Or more likely, someone else.

Which is why on that day, for the record, she wore green, just like envy.

∾

CHAPTER TWO

Six months earlier

William lifted the small envelope from his desk and turned it over in his hands. He studied the handwriting on the front. It was familiar; it was the handwriting that had been etched on his heart. *Hers.*

Running his fingertip along the edges, he felt the rush he typically got when it came to Addison. He swallowed hard, the uneasy feeling returned. In an instant, he knew that she knew. Or maybe not, he hoped. Maybe it was just the guilt eating at him. Either way, something about her that morning had seemed off— now, he was quite certain— this was it. His cover had been blown. *Why else would she send him a handwritten note?*

It had been a long time since she'd resorted to this method of communication. That's how he knew. *Something was off.*

She never sent letters when things were going well and things between the two of them had been great. Better than ever. *Except for the tiny little secret he kept from her, that is.*

Mostly, they were still figuring each other out, having settled into their second month of married life. It didn't make a lot of sense, not to him but something significant had shifted, it seemed, the moment they'd said their *I Do's,* and he didn't know if it was meant to be that way or not— but it was. More importantly, something had changed within him when he became somebody's husband. It was as though a small rift, a tiny crack formed, and it was one he was working to repair. *For her.* For them. Their marriage meant more than anything to him, and he was determined, that even if all else failed, *this* relationship would be the one thing that he'd get right in his life. No matter what it took, no matter what he had to do to keep it that way.

This was supposed to be the best time of their lives. *'The honeymoon period.'* Only William didn't believe in honeymoon periods and it was exactly six weeks after the wedding when things got tricky. He'd attended a business dinner solo, he hadn't wanted to go without her, and he'd said as much, but she was busy with business of her own. Perhaps that was where it all started. As circumstance would have it, he ran into one of his stepfather's former business associates that night. She hadn't been there to witness the shift, to see what the past could do to him, the way it could bring him to his knees, if he let it. Until that night, any change that might have occurred in him had hardly been noticeable. From the outside, anyway. William hadn't seen the man in years, though he recognized him immediately. As if on cue, his happiness faded and the empty feeling returned. Still, he steered clear. He'd planned to duck out early to get home to his beautiful wife anyhow, she always knew what to do to fill the void. But as fate would have it, the man intercepted him at the door.

He tapped his shoulder. "William."

William turned, knowing exactly who he'd see standing behind him. "James."

The man extended his hand. "I heard about the Gleason merger."

William feigned surprise. "Oh, yeah?"

"It's impressive," James said, patting him on the back.

William clenched his jaw. He didn't like people putting their hands on him. "Thanks."

"Looks like that old man of yours really made something out of you, huh?" the man added and that was it. There they were, words, floating between them, hanging in the air, at once setting everything, all of the progress he'd made, in a backward motion. *The way people can so easily bring words to life.*

William bit his tongue so hard it bled. It was better than the alternative, knocking the guy out. *Too many witnesses.* His attorneys would be all over him for it, the event being so public and all. Nonetheless, there were a million responses he could've followed with. But it had taken him a long time to understand that most things can be said in silence. So, he merely shook his head, excused himself, and stepped out into the warm night air.

~

UPON RETURNING HOME, HE FOUND ADDISON ASLEEP AND against his better judgment, he decided to wake her. Not slowly, and not calmly. All at once. He wanted her. He had to have her. He pulled up her nightie and fucked her in a way he hadn't in months. It was hard and rough, fast and abrupt. He was distant, somewhere far off, both inside himself and outside, not really there, and yet completely there. She took note. He wondered later whether that kind of fucking was too much for someone who was now your wife—someone who, as a husband, you'd vowed to love and protect. But then, he hadn't exactly remembered her complaining.

Later, in the early morning hours, tangled up in sweat and each other, the nightmares returned after a long hiatus. William half-expected it. After all, the unrelenting pressure that precedes the rest had returned. Although, perhaps looking back, he realized the pressure had been building, only now, it was magnified ten-fold.

That's the thing about love. You can get lost in it. But you can't stay lost forever.

~

FROM THE NIGHT OF THE BUSINESS DINNER ON, HE BEGAN seeing things—things he hadn't seen before— things he wasn't sure whether were real or imagined. Movie reels played in his mind, and he wasn't sure if it were memories, long buried, he was watching, or events that had actually occurred. Whatever they were they'd come out of the blue, hitting without warning, hard and fast. It started with him conjuring up images of Scott Hammons beating Addison. His powerlessness over it all making him physically ill. The images appeared as sudden flashes of light, a remembrance of all things dark. It evolved from there, he saw injuries his stepfather had imposed upon him—and the damage both men had done played over and over in his mind. Relentlessly. Then, seemingly overnight, the nightmares evolved into daydreams, and before long, they'd begun occurring so randomly and so frequently that he found it tough to get through a conversation without having to excuse himself.

That was when he knew it was time to call Sondra.

He knew from the beginning Addison wouldn't approve, which is why he hadn't asked her permission. He couldn't.

For one, he simply wasn't that kind of man. And two, he didn't want her to know. William Hartman was known to the world as the type of man who took care of his problems. Regardless of what his wife thought, this was just what he intended to do. *What she didn't know wouldn't kill her.*

He and Sondra met once in a place she'd recommended. She didn't need to ask questions, she hadn't asked why—the way Addison would have. She knew.

"Don't hold back," he'd said. "Just no visible marks."

Sondra raised a brow, and he knew it was her way of asking about Addison without actually doing so.

He swallowed hard and looked away. "I'll handle it…" he assured her, rolling his neck. "First, I need to feel something."

Sondra nodded reassuringly. That was all she needed. He liked that about her. He always had.

"I need to know what's real…" he added, a clear warning to stop with the unasked questions. But also, a plea.

"You'll know," was all she'd said in return, and although he didn't understand exactly what she meant, it wouldn't take long before it became apparent.

～

It wasn't that his wife was blind. Not by a long shot. She had asked about the bruises here and there, but he always had a ready answer. His answers were good. Clean, and clear-cut. Also, Sondra was careful. She charged him more for it, but by god, she did the job.

In different times, Addison might have questioned him more, she might have prodded, but at the time, as he would later realize, she had a different agenda altogether.

William's phone rang bringing him back to the present moment. He'd been in one of those far off places he often found himself going these days. He checked the number on the screen, silenced the ringer and then, pulled the card from the envelope.

His hands shook slightly. They did this sometimes when he hadn't slept and today he was running on fumes. It was the nightmares mostly, but also his anxiety about falling asleep. Usually he could control the shaking. Apparently, not today. It didn't help the tremors, holding the note in his hands. Now, he was certain the happiest days of his life were behind him. She was calling him out via a letter. That was their way, it always had been, and the only way Addison would go about it. This was a clue. It was the beginning of the end. Addison had found him out, she knew about his lies. She would flee, and he had given her the rope in which to hang him. *The promise of forever and all his love.* And if it weren't the secrets he kept that would kill his marriage, surely it would be the guilt.

Running his finger along the edge, he felt the paper slice through his skin. It hurt. The slightest hint of relief it brought with it made the pain worthwhile. Now that she'd seen the truth about him, he could let go. He loved her—more than anything. But it was apparent, he wasn't fit to be someone's husband. He wasn't cut from that sort of cloth. He couldn't let her in and it was the keeping her out that would do him in. If nothing else, at least he would be free from the lies. William checked his watch and considered phoning her. It was pointless though. She was on a plane right now headed to Denver, she wouldn't get the call. Anyway, he had time to figure out his next move, how to make a clean break, if there were such a thing. She wasn't due back until tomorrow. *Or maybe never. But for now, he still had time to think. He would come up with something. He always did. He would fly to Denver. He would apologize, he would fix this.*

He watched as blood pooled where the paper had cut

him. He touched his opposite finger to it, widening the cut. Then forced himself to read her words.

Dear William,

Roses are red

Violets are blue

Just like the lines on the pregnancy test I took this morning

Of which there were two.

Happy two months.

Love,

Addison

P.S. I wanted to tell you in person, but I'm flying out this afternoon and won't get in until late tomorrow. :(And, well, you know how bad we are when it comes to keeping secrets from each other.

P.P.S. I didn't expect it to happen so quickly... but then— I always knew we were over-achievers. xx

William exhaled slowly and then all at once. He folded the note, and then ran his fingers through his hair realizing he'd been both right and wrong. *She didn't know.*

Trouble was, this was worse. *He was going to be a father.* He was going to have a child of his own. And what did that mean if he couldn't even get the husband thing right?

One thing was for sure—life as he knew it was over. He'd have to figure this out and soon. There had always been so much at stake. This had been the reason for the lies in the first place. But now... there was going to be another person thrown into the mix. *A baby.*

The thought made him both terrified and elated—more so than he'd ever been.

Which only meant one thing.

He had to see Sondra.

~

CHAPTER THREE

Her mother brought her clothes and not much else. There was nothing left to give, she supposed. After all, the light in her mother's eyes had gone out long ago. But Lydia cared little about that, truthfully. That day, she wore the color brown from head to toe because she understood that when it comes to psychology, brown relates to the hardworking, to those who are industrious and reliable—to those who have both feet planted firmly on the ground.

Brown was a color she wore often in the early days of their love story. She writes to him so he will know all about it. She wants him to understand her, to know the depth of who she is. And he will. She will stop at nothing because reliability and hard work, Lydia has decided, are things she and William have in common. To prove it, she spends her days doing little else but writing to him. How else will he know?

9:14 AM

Dearest William,

31

For three months, following your little rendezvous on the news, I'd been trying to figure out a way to get close to you. Really close. Not like the times in the coffee shops where I sat and watched you come and go—or where we were seated side by side in restaurants, and yet still lifetimes apart.

That was enough for a while.

I told myself it had to be. I was watching you. Studying you. It filled me up to learn all about you. I learned how you took you coffee, your go-to lunch options, right down to the way you often snuck out of business dinners to call *her*. I was watching, always watching and I saw it all. I saw the way you'd sneak off to a dark corner somewhere. You'd talk filthy to her, and judging by your response—by the way you sometimes had to adjust yourself afterward, and then wait several minutes before returning to the table, she must have done the same.

The last time I watched this little escapade occur, I wanted to go to you. To help you out. I wanted to finish you off. And I almost did. I almost went through with it, finally, but as I rounded the corner, you caught my eye, and I saw something in you then. You were startled. It was you in a way I hadn't seen you before. Something told me I had to wait. To be patient. You weren't ready, not yet.

But there was more. I saw a weakness there. A weakness I hadn't seen before.

That weakness, it seemed, was her.

It was then I knew just what had to be done.

I had to get closer. Not just to you, but to her.

I had to go deeper, further than I thought.

I had to become her.

Kisses,

L

~

ASIDE FROM HER MOTHER, LYDIA HAD A SECOND VISITOR THAT day as well. Things went okay, but not great. Just like the rest of them—the woman took what she wanted (a timeline of events more or less) and once she was satisfied, she did what everyone else did, she tossed Lydia aside.

It was okay, though. Because Lydia had gotten what she wanted.

She'd gotten another letter to him.

3:12 PM

Dear William,

I realized what had to be done. Mission: Become Addison, that is. I applied to your company. Then I applied to your wife's company. I studied them the way I studied you. I learned more about business than I ever wanted to know. After I had applied, I followed up at regular two-week intervals on the dot. I proved in those emails that I was a fit for whatever you had in mind. But for three whole months, my emails went unanswered. Nothing but canned responses. Typical, I must say.

And honestly, that was the first thing I would change—and I told you as much at the time. Or rather, I told the bots pretending to be you, anyway. I mean… what is wrong with companies these days? Is nothing personal anymore?

Well, I tell you what, William. This was personal!

And eventually my hard work paid off. Three months in… I finally got a response. I got an interview! With none other than your wife herself. *Finally!*

You of all people should know that persistence pays. Also, patience apparently.

I waltzed into that interview more prepared than I'd been my entire life. I knew everything about everything. I learned the staffing and hospitality industry inside out and upside down. I knew your wife's goals and what she was trying to accomplish. I knew the way she took her coffee and what time she came and went. I knew about mirroring body language and tone of voice. Because I'd watched her. Just like I watched you. It's pretty easy to tail a person when you know what you're doing and if you're careful. I'd been doing it my whole life. Thanks to my expert skill, I even knew what she'd be wearing for our little person-to-person chat.

And, so... I matched it, fairly closely with a few minor exceptions—after all, one has to differentiate just a little! I dressed in Navy, as did she—to signify that we are team players. It was her choice, obviously. But I would've chosen it, too! Because it's a color of confidence, and I know you're into that sort of thing.

Spoiler alert: I got the job. Of course, I did.

But then, you know that by now.
Your wife was quite taken with me...
And I knew you would be, too.
Only it wasn't what I knew then that counted.
It was what I didn't know.

Yours truly,
L

P.S. I wrote you a little something:
Sometimes I wonder
In our quest to be known
If we give too much away.

ADDISON RETURNED FROM DENVER SICKER THAN SICK. SHE'D

known morning sickness, sure, but never this early, even with the twins. William had flown out to Denver to care for her, and she wasn't sure she'd ever seen him so worried or so attentive. She hadn't wanted to tell him about the pregnancy in a letter, but truth be told, she wasn't quite sure how he would take the news, and she couldn't face him if he wasn't as happy as she was.

Over the past few months, ever since the wedding, come to think of it, he'd been distracted—a bit off, but she chalked it up to the merger. She knew he hadn't been sleeping. That's why he'd started practicing martial arts again, to give him an outlet. Only, it didn't help, not as far as she could see. He only came home injured which seemed to both balance and unsettle him. She mentioned it once, and he hadn't taken well to her observation, so she decided it was best if she didn't say a lot about it. She simply observed from a distance and offered help where she could, which was usually in their bedroom—or wherever— if the boys weren't home. Hence the quick pregnancy. Sex was their love language and always had been. Still, it had gotten rougher and more intense lately. More like it had been in the beginning. Not that she was complaining, she wasn't. It's just that something shifted. It was as though they were trying to save themselves in the act, and looking back, maybe they were.

But now that she'd told him about the baby, in the matter of a few days, he had gone back to his usual old self. To the man she'd always known. Right down to trying to control everything.

This was what Addison was thinking as she leaned over the toilet and hurled once again.

After a few minutes of praying the last time was the last time, and she could finally pull herself up and get to work, she felt William as he leaned over her and smoothed the damp hair away from her face. "Like I said, I think you need to hire someone."

So, this is how this is going to go. She looked up at him, wiped her chin, and rested her head against the coolness of the porcelain. "Why… women aren't capable of handling work and growing a baby?"

He sat down on the bathroom floor beside her. "Addison, come on… Look at you. You can barely lift your head."

"I'm aware of how I feel…"

"Yes. But are you *sure* this is normal? I don't care what the doctor says—"

"The doctors say it's better than normal. They say it's a sign of a healthy pregnancy…" she told him with a sigh. "You heard them yourself."

His mouth formed a hard line. He wasn't going to argue with her. His mind was made up. "Just hire someone, Addison," he said. "Or I will."

She wanted to object, to raise her voice, and put him in his place, but all she could do was lean her head over the side of the toilet and dry heave in to the bowl once more. William rubbed her back in long slow circles until the latest round subsided. *No matter how many times you've been pregnant, you never forget that feeling. Or how much you'd give anything to make it stop. Her stomach felt like an ocean, and she was in a tiny rowboat trying to fight the current of a hurricane.*

Once she could speak again, she sat up slowly, studied his face, and uttered the words she knew he wanted to hear. *This one wasn't about winning.* She'd take one for the team. In fact, she already had. They were supposed to be happy and she was too sick to fight anyway. "For your information," she relented. "I have an interview scheduled today."

He smiled and kissed the top of her head.

"One step ahead of me… as usual." He stood and extended his hand.

She took his hand and he pulled her up slowly. He steadied her, searched her eyes to make sure the sickness had receded and then he wrapped his arms around her, pulled her to him, and hugged her tight. "I'm sorry, Addison."

She frowned knowing he couldn't see her face. "For what?"

William inhaled and then let the breath out slowly. "I just feel like saying it, okay?"

She exhaled. "Okay."

And all of a sudden, it was.

~

CHAPTER FOUR

Already late to meet her friend Jess, Addison frantically searched for keys. She texted to say she was running late, as she'd had to excuse herself twice in the interview she'd just conducted in order to throw up. *Why they called it morning sickness, she'd never know.* Jess would understand.

Finally, she breathed a sigh of relief. Addison spotted the shiny metallic of the car keys just underneath her desk where they'd likely fallen in one of her desperate attempts to make it to the ladies room as the bile rose in her throat, threatening to spill over. She took a deep breath, sat down in her chair and paused for a moment, before letting out a long exhale. *Things would get better now.*

It wasn't her usual style, typically she wasn't impulsive, but she'd hired the woman on the spot. She wasn't sure if it was because she liked her as much as it was that she was desperate to have some relief. Desperate or not, she was pretty sure she'd made the right decision. There was something about the woman that was familiar. She dressed well and played the part. Most of all, she was quick. It would help that she was sharp because Addison was tired, and her boss, Sondra, would be happy that everything would now be taken care of. Particularly, in a timeframe she approved of.

It seemed like the perfect fit. Later, she would come to realize—the perfect storm.

Checking the time on her phone, Addison stood slowly. Immediately, she wanted to sit back down. She wanted to sleep. She clutched her head and then her stomach. She was lightheaded, and the very idea of food appalled her. Still, she couldn't cancel lunch. Jess was going through a tough time and had finally agreed to leave the house—so the last thing Addison wanted to do was to cancel on her and mess up the small amount of progress she knew she'd fought hard to gain.

They ended up meeting in a cafe down the street from Addison's office, and when she arrived, the cafe was already bustling with the usual lunch crowd. The smell of food overwhelmed her as she scanned the room. She located Jess seated in a corner booth, head down, typing away on her laptop.

Just then, as if she'd sensed it, Jess closed her computer, looked up, met Addison's eye, and smiled. She smiled back. *Thank God. She came.* It was good to see her friend up, out of the house, dressed in something other than overpriced sweats—and not to mention, working again.

She made her way over to the table. Jess slid out from the booth, stood, and hugged her. When she pulled back, she eyed Addison up and down. "How are you feeling?" she asked quizzically. "You look absolutely green."

Addison's mouth formed a hard line. She scooted into the booth seat. Jess followed suit opposite her. "In that case..." she answered. "About like I look. I really don't think I've *ever* felt this bad."

Jess chuckled. "You have. You were pretty sick with the twins, remember?"

"I try not to," Addison replied offering a faint smile. She studied her friend, pleased to see she'd made an effort, the way she used to, even going as far as to apply makeup. "You look good."

Jess waved her off. "I'm okay. But that's not why I'm here. I want to know about *you*..."

"For the book?"

Jess frowned. "No, for my sanity."

Addison pursed her lips.

"SO—he flew out to meet you—which I assume means he took the baby news well." She took a sip of her water and placed the glass down. "Not that I expected any less..."

Addison smiled a real smile then. The kind that lit up her whole face. "He's genuinely happy. And aside from being so sick..." she said, glancing toward the door and then back at her friend. "I'm over the moon, too."

Jess grinned. "Well, I hate to say it... but I told you so."

A waitress appeared then and hastily demanded their orders. Jess ordered a salad and soup. But all Addison could stomach was hot tea with lemon and crackers. *If even that. It still remained to be seen.*

"I still can't believe you're pregnant."

"*You* can't..."

"Not that I hadn't expected it at some point, I guess..."

"What do you mean?"

"It's just that... I thought we'd already been there, done that. Raised our families simultaneously, I mean. And now here you are...You're starting over... and I guess... so am I—in a sense." Jess paused and looked down at the table then. "Just in a completely different way."

Addison placed her hand on top of her friend's and squeezed. "Oh, Jess. I'm sorry if—"

"Mrs. Hartman?"

Both Jess and Addison looked up in surprise. Addison cocked her head and raised her brow. She was surprised to see the woman she'd just interviewed standing opposite them. "Lydia."

"I'm so sorry to interrupt. I was just having lunch and was on my way out, and well, I looked up and there you were. What a coincidence!" the woman said animatedly, her pitch ten times too high.

Addison glanced at Jess, who gave her a look. She extended her hand. Jess had never been one to hide the way she felt. Until lately, that is. "I'm Jessica and you are—" she'd said, her tone sharp and inquisitive.

Addison shook her head, sighed, and tried to intercept Jess and her mood. "Gosh, I'm sorry. How rude of me. Jessica, this is Lydia. As of about an hour ago, I brought her on board at the agency as my new right-hand woman."

Lydia smiled. "It's a pleasure."

"That it is," Jess said.

She and her new assistant exchanged a few words, about what, Addison couldn't remember, as she was too focused on the way Jess studied Lydia. It made Addison look at Lydia in a way she hadn't before. Her jet-black hair stood in vast comparison to her pale skin and her eyes were a shade of brown so light they were almost cat-like. Her appearance was striking in many ways, and while she wasn't overtly beautiful, she definitely had an exotic look about her. She wore a navy blue dress, not unlike the one Addison wore. Finally, Lydia stopped talking and looked at Jess.

"It was nice to meet you Jessica—" she'd said, her voice low.

"Likewise," Jessica replied, and then the two of them watched the woman turn and exit the cafe without looking back.

Addison spoke first. "You didn't like her."

Jessica shook her head. "Oh... I don't know—"

"Jess, this is me you're talking to."

"Why in the world would you hire someone like *her?*"

"I'm not sure what you mean," Addison said grinning.

Jess exhaled. "For one, I don't like her energy. And her appearance says she's trying pretty hard at something. What, I'm not sure..."

Addison laughed. "Well, aren't you just a ray of sunshine today. And you're worried about *her* energy?"

Jess pursed her lips and took a sip of her water before replying. "She's got a lot, that's for sure."

Addison rolled her eyes and looked toward the door. "You mean she's peppy? That's one thing I like about her actually... I *so* need peppy right now."

Jess shook her head. "No, what I mean is if she's going to be your assistant, then she's bound to be pretty involved in your life. I'm just surprised that *that* is what you want."

"Yeah..." Addison said, glancing back at her friend. "But you don't understand, Jess. She knew everything about everything. I mean... you could tell she *really* did her homework. It's almost as if exactly what I needed just appeared right out of thin air at precisely the right time."

"Okay."

"I get it. Yeah, sure, she's a little high strung. But, like I said... she really knows her stuff. And I need that right now. I'm exhausted."

Jess sighed. "Be careful, Addison. You know that old saying..."

"Which one?"

"All of them. But mostly, be careful what you wish for."

"I am careful."

"I don't think she's a good fit."

"Well, it's a good thing *you're* not the one who hired her."

Jess held her palms up and then let them rest on the table. "I don't get it... I really don't. It's just you're always so hell bent on learning the hard way."

"I am not."

Jess didn't argue. She smiled faintly. Addison looked away.

And they'd both left it at that.

~

OF COURSE, LYDIA HAD TO LEARN THE HARD WAY THAT SHE'D only been hired because the worst possible thing ever had happened. How could it be that the love of her life had gone and knocked up his wife? Maybe that wouldn't sound so abnormal to most people—but Lydia wasn't most people. She knew the truth. Addison had gotten pregnant on purpose. To keep him. William didn't even want the baby. She had practically heard the words come straight from the horse's mouth.

She had followed Addison to lunch, parked herself in an adjacent booth—which was no easy feat seeing that it was already occupied. But she worked her usual charm, landed a seat, and listened.

Sadly, what she overheard was quite possibly the worst news she'd heard in her entire life. She wanted to go to Addison then, to stab her fifty times, and make sure at least half of them went straight to the heart just like she'd done to her.

But Lydia was smarter than that. She knew all about timing. She knew her plan had to be calculated. So, when she couldn't take it anymore, she did what any person in her shoes would have done. She sauntered up to the table and played herself up.

Addison was pleasant enough, but that company of hers

needed to be the first thing on Lydia's list to knock off. *Where there's a will, there's a way.*

Later that day, she needed a release. All of her anger and her hurt had been bottled up, and it was an outlet she sought. She traced a W into her skin. She wanted to write his name all over her body, to bathe herself in him. And when that wasn't enough, she used a paperclip she'd nabbed from Addison's office to carve the letter into her thigh. She etched it slowly. The pain she felt was a relief. It felt good to see the dark red of her blood drip down across the backdrop of her pale thigh. As she watched the dark liquid bubble to the surface and spill over, she got a brilliant idea. She would make her pain worth something. She would make someone else see the beauty in it. And, so it was in her own blood that she crafted her first correspondence to William.

William Hartman *would* love *her*. He would impregnate *her* with his baby. It wouldn't be an accident. It would be magic. This was the only way for her now. Once Lydia set her sights on something, she was like a pit bull lunging at its victim's throat. *That's what her father always used to say, anyway.*

Dearest William,

I've found my way in—and in that, we will find each other.
It will be magic.

XX,
YOUR NUMBER ONE FAN

P.S. Speaking of magic—I wrote a little something just for you...

Magic.
Once you've tasted magic like this.

Then, you know—

Everything else is second rate.

And nothing less will do.

So best eat it up...

For there's more where that came from.

~

CHAPTER FIVE

William sat adjacent to his board members as he tried to focus on the task at hand. It wasn't easy, something was pulling at him. He was a puppet on a string and someone, somewhere held the string, and was happily dancing a jig with his concentration.

He adjusted and then loosened his tie as he half-listened to the PowerPoint presentation on the screen. While he was there physically in the boardroom, his mind was back in a different time, in a different room altogether.

"Hand me the belt." The booming voice demanded.

William didn't budge.

"Damn it, boy. I said HAND ME THE BELT."

He stared at the belt lying at his stepfather's feet, but he didn't make a move for it.

"Well, well... it looks like someone has finally decided to stop being such a little pussy."

William stared at the floor. He refused to take his eyes off the belt.

It would be the first time he'd understand the importance of always looking a person in the eye.

His stepfather let out a long laugh and then hurled his tumbler across the room, hitting William in the head. He sunk to the floor and rocked back and forth, his palm pressed to the gaping wound just above his hairline. Blood poured from underneath his hand onto the hardwood floor.

"Now look what you've done! You've made a fucking mess out of my parlor!" his stepfather slurred and spat. He shook his head in disbelief and then stood and walked past William. He must have changed his mind because he turned back and kicked William hard enough that it knocked the wind out of him. He took two steps toward the door. William gathered his knees to make himself as small as possible, he was aware of what came next, only to find his stepfather would have mercy on him that day. He lowered his tone. "You are a six-year-old nobody, son. Do you hear me? A nothing! Your own father didn't want you. Your mother doesn't even want you—if she did… don't you think it would be her here disciplining you?" He threw his arms in the air waving them around as though he were urging on a crowd that wasn't there. "Noooo," he slurred. "Of course not. It's too much for her," he laughed, motioning toward William. He coughed and almost choked on his words. "Face it, kid," he said. "No one wants you."

In the end, it had taken eight stitches to sew up his head. That was the last and only time William refused to pick up that belt.

"Mr. Hartman." The man raised his voice. "Excuse me, Mr. Hartman?"

William shook his head, tried to refocus. Finally, his mind brought him back to the present. He paused and looked the board member in the eye. He took a deep breath as he realized he'd been pacing.

All eyes were on him.

"Are you all right? You were mumbling to yourself—"

William cocked his head. When he spoke, his voice was harsh, a clear warning. "I'm fine."

Paul, his latest assistant, stood. "All right, everyone," he announced. "Let's take ten."

William watched as people quickly dispersed with their eyes either on the floor or their phones.

When the room was empty, he slunk down into his chair and ran his fingers through his hair. Suddenly, his palms were wet. For a moment, he panicked thinking it was blood. He rose and shot for the door.

"William. William!" Paul called after him.

He stopped at the door. "I'm bleeding," he said, holding up his hands. He could feel the color drain from his face.

Paul frowned and considered what he'd said for a moment. He shook his head. "You're sweating. Not bleeding."

William exhaled and stared at his hands in disbelief. *No blood.*

"You don't look well," Paul exclaimed. "Maybe you're coming down with something... Why don't I clear your schedule for the afternoon?"

William shook his head slightly. "No. Just give me two hours. Move a few things around if you need to, but I'll be back by two."

Paul eyed him and nodded.

William turned and took his phone from his pocket and opened the text. *I need to see you. Now.* He hit the send button before he could question himself.

A few seconds later, a response: *Give me thirty and meet me at the usual spot.*

He read her words back and exhaled in relief.

~

WILLIAM MET SONDRA IN AN OLD ABANDONED BUILDING ON

the east side of town, just off the highway. He was running late due to trying to locate parking. It was a mistake driving his silver Bugatti. Attempting to find an inconspicuous place to park proved pretty much impossible on that side of town. *He should have gotten his driver to bring him.* But then he would have had to admit to security that he wasn't in his office napping. Also, desperate times called for desperate measures.

He knew Sondra wouldn't be pleased with his tardiness, and sure enough, she was already waiting when he arrived.

His pulse quickened as he spotted her, hands on her hips, blank expression on her face. William simply nodded as he walked to the middle of the room where an old wooden barstool sat. For a second, he wondered how such a thing ended up in a place like this, but then he realized she must have brought it along. The building was empty, save for the two of them, it was sparse and damp. The air felt sticky and smelled faintly of beer and overwhelmingly of warm, wet piss.

Once he'd reached the barstool, Sondra walked over and kissed him on each cheek. She was all business as usual—her hair up in a neatly twisted bun. She was dressed in a tight black knee-length dress and five-inch heels. She stepped back and took him in. "You look like shit."

"Thank you for coming," was all he'd said in response. It was all he wanted to say.

She pursed her lips. He knew what she was going to say.

"We can't keep meeting like this, William. You know as well as I do, that eventually, you're going to have to deal with what's going on—"

"Stop," he interrupted, holding one palm up. "Not now—OKAY?"

"William—"

"I'm not in the mood for a lecture—" he said, cutting her

off. "And anyway, we both know that therapy is not why I come here."

"But you did so well for such a long time..."

William clenched his jaw. "Like I said, if I wanted a therapist, I'd go to fucking therapy."

Sondra smiled, and it was the kind that warmed you from the inside.

Then she took two steps forward and backhanded him so hard, he spat blood. He couldn't be sure whether he saw it coming or not. She, just like his stepfather, was often unpredictable.

He tried to recover but she grabbed him by his hair, before letting go once she had his hands where she wanted them. She placed them behind his back and duct taped them together. William waited nervously as she walked circles around him, not once, but twice, admiring her handy work. When she made her way back around behind him, she spread her fingers through his hair and yanked his head backward. When his neck could stretch no further, she leaned in and whispered in his ear all the things he'd so desperately needed to hear. Once she'd finished assaulting him verbally, she followed up with a few blows to the gut and one to the mouth.

"Watch your mouth in my presence, Mr. Hartman. You should know better than to interrupt me when I'm speaking. Hopefully, this will help—" she said, before she slapped him once more, this time so hard his teeth chattered. He slid off the stool slowly. Satisfied, she then left him panting and bleeding on the concrete floor.

He watched her as she walked away, and for just a moment, he felt sick as the realization took over. He wished it had been his wife.

This was supposed to make him feel better.

But it didn't. *What kind of man went to another woman for*

comfort, anyway?

The losing kind, William decided. That's who.

~

WILLIAM GLANCED FROM SIDE TO SIDE AS HE WALKED BACK TO the parked car, in part surprised to see it still sitting there untouched. He hadn't really cared one way or another. Mostly, it was his safety that concerned him, especially now that he was to be a father. He could never be too careful, he realized. Even with Scott Hammons dead. There'd always be another psychopath to take his place. There always had been. That was one thing this lifestyle guaranteed. Not to mention, there was also the possibility of being seen, not too many cars of his kind were seen around this part of town, so it wouldn't be too hard to figure his identity out given the small percentage of people who owned Bugattis.

Also, Sondra was right. They couldn't keep meeting here. For one, it was too hard for him to get away from security—they always gave him shit, but in the end, he was the boss. Two, it was dangerous, and before long, he'd likely find himself in a situation where he no longer needed her at all.

As he clicked the button on his keychain, he checked his surroundings once more for good measure. A note taped to his windshield caught his eye. *Motherfucker.* Knowing the rules better than to pause to grab it, he deftly got into his car, started it, and took off.

Once he was a few blocks away, and certain he wasn't being tailed, he let the window down, reached out, grabbed it, and tossed it into the passenger seat where it sat until he pulled into the garage back at the office.

William pulled into his parking space, killed the ignition and sat for a moment trying to collect his thoughts. He cleaned the dried blood from his face and then laid his head against the smooth steering wheel. Suddenly, a tap on his window startled him. He sat up and found himself staring at his wife.

He pushed the button to let the passenger window down. "Hasn't anyone warned you about hanging out in parking garages?" She smiled a devilish smile, and all at once, William missed her more than he had in his entire life.

"Get in."

She furrowed her brow. "Okay, but only for a minute… I've got a meeting in an hour… and my new assistant is meeting me there ahead of time."

William walked around to the passenger side, and opened the door. His breath caught when she reached down and lifted the note off the passenger seat. He hadn't yet read it and worried it might be a flyer of some sort that would give away his whereabouts. He worried that he'd have to explain. He climbed in the passenger seat and motioned for her to straddle him.

She raised her brow. "Seriously?"

He shrugged and eyed the note in her hand. "You're wearing a skirt."

She glanced down at her attire. "Addison, get in the car."

She smiled. He took the note from her hand and positioned her appropriately. "You do realize you're going to have to get a bigger car if we're going to keep meeting this way…"

This time, he smiled. "Only temporarily."

"Where've you been anyway?" she asked nonchalantly.

"Lunch."

She bit her lip. *God, he wanted her. Now.* "Your lip is bleeding—"

William swallowed. "I bit it," he said, then cleared his throat. Addison eyed him suspiciously. Talking wasn't what he had in mind. He placed a finger over her lips, and then leaned forward and kissed her urgently. She kissed back so hard it made his mouth hurt, so he pulled away and then trailed his lips down her neck as he pulled her skirt over her hips. He raised her up slightly, slid her panties to the side, and slipped one finger into the warmth of her. She looked around and then back at him, minimally appalled. Mostly, it was for show. She was good at that part. "William," she chided. "Not here—"

He covered her mouth with his and kissed her softly. "I need you... Anyway, the windows are blacked out..."

He was the kind of man who knew what he wanted and took it, and that's exactly what he intended to do. Here and now. He pushed his finger in deeper, and then slowly withdrew it, before pushing forward once more, harder this time, knowing all too well what she could and couldn't resist.

"William—" she'd panted, both wanting to resist and wanting to give in at the same time. He trailed his mouth down her neck and back up once more, as he undid his belt and freed himself from his pants. He listened to the sound of her voice vaguely plead once more. It pleased him that he knew how to work her over. *He always had known how to make her say his name.*

He pulled back slightly and searched her eyes for a yes. When he'd gotten it, he slowly removed his finger and replaced it with something better. And there in that garage, in the front seat of his inconspicuous car, he fucked her slow and steady, and all the while, she begged for more in the form of repeating his name over and over. By the time he finished, she was breathless, and they both knew he'd given her everything he had.

It was all he'd ever wanted.

And more.

~

CHAPTER SIX

A ddison perched herself atop the crinkled cold paper of the exam table. She took out her phone and nervously attempted to distract herself. She glanced at the screen and then around the exam room at photos of new mothers with healthy babies. She was worried she might not make it into the same club.

She took a deep breath and willed herself to be wrong. *Just this once, please, let me be wrong.*

She thought about texting Jess, but the thought almost made the situation she faced seem too real and the image on the screen was too blurry to see anyhow. Instead, she rested the phone in her lap and silently pleaded with William to hurry. Not normally one to need to call on her husband when she was in trouble, she realized something is very wrong with her, and this time it wasn't just the nausea. She knew he would want to be there. He would want to know.

As the dizziness took over, she relented and gently lowered herself backward onto the table, curled into a ball, and silently prayed he would get there soon. *He would make this all right.*

She closed her eyes and pictured herself elsewhere until a quiet knock at the door brought her attention back to the present from somewhere deep inside herself. When she opened her eyes, she found her new assistant standing beside her.

"I wanted to check on you... The nurse said the doctor is on his way back from a delivery and should be here shortly. And Mr. Hartman just texted to say he's right around the corner."

Addison nodded and let her eyes fall closed again. "Something's wrong. I can feel it."

She felt the woman brush her hair away from her face. "Shhh," she whispered. "Now, now...it's all going to be all right..."

But Addison knew her assistant was wrong. She'd just felt a warm wet gush between her legs as though confirmation were in order. She sat up then as the door opened, and her husband walked through, his face pale and pained with worry.

"I'm bleeding."

William sighed and took a look around the room. "What did the doctor say?"

"She hasn't seen him yet," her assistant said hurriedly. "He's on his way back from a delivery."

William set his jaw and went for the door. "What do you mean she hasn't seen him yet?"

Addison listened as he called out and demanded the nurse get a doctor in there now.

"William," Addison said, her voice cracking. "Calm down."

He looked at Addison and then back at the woman. "Why in the hell did you bring her *here*?"

"William," Addison warned.

Lydia's face dropped. "I-I..."

"She was just doing what I told her," Addison assured

him. She squeezed her eyes shut. Then she shifted and winced. The cramping worsened, and so she curled farther into the fetal position and she cradled her stomach. The door opened once more. *If that wasn't a doctor, they were in trouble for her husband was about two point five seconds from causing a scene.*

"I'm Dr. Calvart," the man said as he shook William's hand and then made his way over to the table. He assessed her visually and then checked the tablet in his hand. "So, you're about nine weeks along, it says here. You've developed some cramping and spotting over the last few hours?"

"Yes," Addison cried. "I think the bleeding has become heavier since I arrived."

The doctor's face twisted but just slightly—although Addison was certain no one in the room missed it. He opened a drawer beneath the examination table, pulled out a gown, and placed it beside her. "Well, some cramping and even bleeding at this stage can be normal, but I think it's best if we take a peek via ultrasound," he said, closing the drawer. "I'll let you get changed, have my nurse wheel the machine in, and I'll be back in a few."

Lydia looked from Addison to William and back at Addison. "I'll just wait out in the waiting room."

"It's okay, Lydia. You can go ahead and head home."

She shook her head but was unable to wipe the worried expression she wore. "I'd like to wait here, if that's okay."

Addison nodded and studied her husband's face as the woman passed him on her way out. Clearly, he was perturbed. It wasn't Lydia's fault. This seemed to be his usual state these days.

Sensing her watching him, he went to Addison and took her hand. "I'm sorry," he promised. "I got here as soon as I could."

She looked away. "I'm pretty sure I've lost the baby."

William flinched. "Let's wait and see what the doctor says."

Tears welled up in her eyes. "I don't need the doctor to tell me what I already know—"

"Let's just wait and see, okay?" His voice was rough.

She swallowed the rebuttal back as he gently wiped the tears from her cheeks. She let him have it. Hope, that is.

Because sometimes in love, it's just what you do.

Even if in the end, she was right.

AS THE FOLLOWING WEEK PASSED, ADDISON'S LIFE LITERALLY became a nightmare overnight. There were doctor appointments followed by doctor appointments and blood work followed by more blood work. For the first few days, the pain was excruciating, and then once the cramps had subsided some, the bleeding became worse than she could recall, ever, even after giving birth.

She told herself she'd take a week off and let her assistant handle things, but the truth was she was dying to get back to work. If nothing more than to get some semblance of normalcy back.

The doctors assured them they could try again. They'd said the miscarriage was considered a fluke medically—or, in other words, that there was no rhyme or reason for it— that sometimes these things just happened.

But for William and Addison, being the kind of people they were, they each took their own share of the blame. On some level, and for different reasons, they each believed they'd played a part in the demise of the pregnancy. No matter what the doctors said.

William swore it was his fault, swore it was the sex he'd insisted upon that afternoon that caused it. While somewhere deep down, Addison told herself it was her inability to set work aside and focus on the baby that had caused it. At other times, she insisted it was the relentless nausea and the meds she'd taken (but only once) to help with it. And maybe, if she'd forced herself to eat even just a little, things would have turned out differently.

Before long, with each passing day, she found a new reason to blame herself.

She knew William felt he was at fault, he'd told her that much, but she hadn't expected him to grieve so differently. He retreated even more than before. He didn't want to talk about it, he'd said. He didn't need to. What happened had happened, and they'd try again.

Once the doctor had assured him they could still have children, he backed off. He saw to it that she had the help she needed and the boys were cared for while she recovered, but other than that, he poured himself into his work.

Addison gave him space.

Only the more she gave, the more he took.

$\sim$

ADDISON STOOD FACING THE MIRROR IN HER BATHROOM. SHE studied her reflection and ran her hands through her matted hair. *It was time to pick herself up. It was time to get back to business.*

She rubbed at her swollen eyelids and tried to figure out where to start. As hard as she'd attempted to focus on her unkempt appearance, it was the wedding photo on the countertop that kept grabbing her attention, calling her back. The photo taunted her. It seemingly forced its way into her hand, insisting she pick it up, face it. She had to stop making this whole thing about her.

Her husband had assured her nothing was wrong, but she

knew differently. Over the past two weeks, he'd taken to sleeping in the guest bedroom so he didn't wake her when he came to bed. She needed her rest in order to recover, he'd insisted. But it wasn't the truth.

Addison looked down at the photo and then back at her reflection in the mirror once more. She certainly wasn't the girl in the picture, not anymore. For one, she'd lost weight. Her face was pale, her cheeks had sunken in. Her frame was gaunt and she looked at least a decade older as of this morning. A stark contrast to the girl in the photo, without a doubt.

As she ran her finger over the cool glass, she studied the expression her husband wore in the photo. While it stung on a visceral level to see the way he looked at her then in comparison to how he'd seemingly glossed over her the past few weeks, she understood that it was time to accept what was. She needed to look at what had once been—in order to understand how to get back there.

Addison smiled as she thought back on her wedding day. She remembered clearly what it felt like to stand barefoot on the beach in nearly the same spot she'd fallen in love with the man who was standing opposite her. She recalled the joy she felt as they whispered vows that she would scarcely remember in the coming months, but vows that had somehow etched themselves into her heart. That was the funny thing about words. They become living, breathing things. They become a part of you.

On the flip side, what Addison realized that morning more than ever were words, just like photographs, could haunt you if you're not careful. They serve as reminders of what once was—and what remained.

And while she may not recall the exact words that she repeated there on the beach six months prior, she did remember other things about that day. She remembered the way the sun warmed the skin across her back. She remembered slipping into the vintage cream dress that now hangs at the back of her closet, and how William had so gently peeled it off later that night. She remembered the way his eyes lit up as she came down the makeshift aisle. Perhaps no one else noticed. But she did.

She remembered the words he'd whispered once they were finally alone, after all of the noise had died down—how he'd told her the dress was beautiful, but that it had nothing on what was underneath. She remembered how the two of them became one that day—in the eyes of the law, at least— and what that felt like. She hadn't wanted to make a commitment of that magnitude, not in the beginning, but she did then. Something stirred in her thinking back on it. She realized that it would take many months, if not years, before either of them truly grasped what this meant in terms of their relationship.

It was a dance, she realized.

But then, maybe, it would always be a dance when it came to the two of them.

She glanced at herself in the mirror and back at the photo.

Her children ran circles around them as their friends looked on, and beyond that, how a small crowd had gathered merely out of curiosity. She remembered the way the ocean looked, calm and steady, as they whispered their I Do's against a backdrop of blue—their toes dug firmly into the sand, as though their feet were foreshadowing all that was to come.

It was a beautiful day full of joy and love and laughter. Although later, and especially on days like this one, there would be many occasions upon which she would think about all the things that no one tells you on your wedding day.

Days where you bled for too many reasons and none at all. Days where it takes all you have just to look in the mirror and face that which you've become. Because if not, if you refused, you realized, there simply wasn't any other way forward.

She wondered what might have happened had she sensed any of what was to come looking at William there on the beach. He grinned and kissed her lips, sealing the deal and she knew she hadn't been thinking about the future at all. She wondered what she might have changed if she could have predicted this, if she could have seen herself as she was today—stripped down bare, both literally and metaphorically.

As she stared at the photo, there was an ever-increasing inclination that the allure of their wedding day, and all it encapsulated, would always be lurking closely in the background, particularly for her husband.

William was a man of high expectations, one who demanded excellence in all areas of his life. Judging by what she saw in the mirror, she'd fallen so far from anything even remotely resembling that. Glancing at her reflection, she feared it was the wedding portrait version of her he craved. Not this. He wanted her the way she was before, the way she was in the photo—a vision of perfection and there was something about that—implied yet not implied that she felt forced to live up to.

Somewhere deep down, she wondered if she would ever again make him as happy as she did standing there on that beach—or whether that was a high they would forever be chasing. After all, *until death do you part,* they'd agreed.

That's not to say they couldn't be happy again. They could. *Couldn't they?*

Addison hoped, with everything she was, with everything

she had, that it was all still there—somewhere, slightly buried underneath the pain and uncertainty of today's reality.

She would pull herself together.

She would make it right again.

Even if it killed her.

~

CHAPTER SEVEN

9:13 AM

Dearest William,

You wanted me.
I wanted you.
It was the beginning,
And the end.
Of everything.

Today, I wear violet, and I write poetry for you. In case you didn't know, violet is a color that allows us to be introspective—to get in touch with deeper feelings. To be fair, I think it is time we both got in touch with our feelings a bit more.

So... I'm going to tell you a little story in hopes that you can understand how very deep mine run.

I didn't want to do it, William.

Really... I didn't.

But when I saw you there with her in the front seat of your car and you were fucking her *like* you *should* have been fucking me, I knew then something had to change. I knew by what I saw that you would appreciate a woman who takes matters into her own hands, a woman who takes charge.

And to tell you the truth, it was easy to be that woman. You may, like the others, think that I'm some loner—that I don't get mine. But that wouldn't be true. Like you, and the color violet, I'm intense. So, you would be wrong, my love. I most certainly do get mine. For starters, I have a fascination with picking up men, a real talent for it, to be sure. Men who are ready and willing to give me what I need. Don't worry—these men, my dear, are *nothing* like you. These men use women to suit their filthy needs. And well, as for me, what can I say? I can't help myself. I'm a woman who likes to play along. I let them win, or at least think they are, and that is why I sometimes do the things I do. Although, that is a story for another day.

For now, I want to tell you about beginnings and endings.

I sometimes see a man who I'll call 'Charlie.' 'Charlie' works at the pharmacy where I pick up my prescriptions (this is also a topic for another day—you see, we have so much to discuss) and I have come to sort of... I guess you could say... *like* Charlie. Charlie is a loner. He is the kind of person people think I am. He's not too smart—which strongly correlates with the amount of pot he smokes, as well as the number of hours he spends playing video games. But who am I to judge? Anyway, one night about six months ago, I waited for 'Charlie' to slip out back, behind the pharmacy for his usual smoke before closing. He didn't seem that surprised to see me, which for a second, threw me off my game. He lit my cigarette. I wasn't even a smoker and while he seemed to know this, he didn't say anything. He could have mentioned it, but he kept his mouth shut. This is how I realized that 'Charlie' was the kind of guy one could come to an understanding with. Anyway, I'd better not get too far ahead of myself. He lit my cigarette, and I returned the favor by giving him the best blowjob of the poor guy's life. I know, because he told me so. The other thing different about 'Charlie' was, unlike the others, when I asked if he wanted my number, he simply smiled and said he already had it. And to think I just mentioned that he wasn't all that smart. Turns out, he was smarter that night than either of us realized.

And roughly, two months and twenty-two fucks later, we would both be glad for that. It was pretty simple, William. That's the part I both love and hate about what I did. I told 'Charlie' I was pregnant.

Then I suggested we use the abortion pill also known as Mifeprex. I know a lot about pharmaceuticals. More on that later—

Anyhow, lo and behold, who do you think was the perfect person to get me what I needed?

You guessed right.

'Charlie.'

Twelve hours later, I crushed it and placed it in the coffee I picked up especially for your wife.

It would get her through the meeting, she'd said.

But she was wrong.

Because what it did a mere two hours later was bring me face to face with you.

Which will certainly go down in history as one of the highlights of my life.

So, I hope you'll understand.

It was necessary.

Not only would it solve the baby problem, it would be a little while before that wife of yours would be fuckable.

And after the way you spoke to me at our first 'official' meeting, I realized you deserved as much.

Sincerely,

L

∼

CHAPTER EIGHT

"This is the third one I've received in two weeks," William said furrowing his brow. "First, the one on my car. Then in my personal mailbox, and now, here in my office... It seems to me this asshole is only getting more brazen."

The man opposite him looked over at his partner and then back at William. "While we can certainly understand your frustration, Mr. Hartman—these letters, unfortunately, aren't anything new. You've been receiving correspondence of this nature for some time, and according to our forensics, they're all likely coming from different sources."

"And?"

"Well—as I mentioned on the phone, my team and I have been over these and feel that... for someone of your stature, this is really nothing out of the ordinary..."

William gritted his teeth. The room had begun to spin, and he felt himself slipping into the familiar black abyss, a feeling he knew all too well lately. "So, what you're telling me is these are simply par for the course?" he asked picking up one of the notes. "Are you saying I'm supposed to just sit here and do nothing?"

"We're not suggesting—"

"No, you're not suggesting—" William said, cutting the consultant off. "You're telling me to tolerate this B.S. when the facts are clear: *whoever* is sending them is *not only* getting more confident, but they're also okay with encroaching on our private property—which to me, speaks volumes given the level of security I employ."

"That's not what we're—"

William slammed his fist on the table, stopping the man mid-sentence. He then swept its contents onto the floor. "Do you have any idea what my family has been through?" He eyed the mess on the floor and then looked up at the men. "I'm paying you decent— no—I'm paying you *good* money to fix this. And here you are asserting these letters, this nonsense is normal?"

"William," Paul pled.

The consultant looked at Paul and then over at William. "No. What I was trying to say is that's not what we are suggesting at all. In fact, I can assure you we are doing everything within our power to contain the situation. In the meantime, I want to make sure we're on the same page here. Didn't you say in our last meeting that your wife had you back off some on the security front?"

William shifted in his seat so that he was able to glare out the window of the high-rise office. "We've made a few changes, sure. But nothing that would allow this—"

The man carefully cut him off. "Well, I think it's time we take another look at where any breaches could be occurring. And again, I want to reiterate that we are doing everything in our power to ensure that this matter is handled swiftly. But if you want my honest opinion—"

William narrowed his gaze and looked directly into the man's eyes. "What else would I be paying you for?"

The man glanced down at the conference room table. "From everything I can see here," he said motioning toward the notes on the floor. "This is likely some minor nut case with a little too much time on his or her hands... someone looking to get their jollies. I realize this isn't helpful considering the circumstances but if I were in your shoes, I would do my best not to be too concerned. While off-putting, it doesn't appear there are any genuine threats being made. And the truth is—it would be difficult to do anything in the legal sense to stop this person, even *if* we knew who he or she was. Being an adoring fan, while annoying and obtrusive, isn't considered breaking the law."

William eyed the man, then stood, walked to the door and opened it. He turned back toward the men. "Not too concerned... huh. This is my family we're talking about. Clearly, we seem to be on different pages." He motioned toward the door. "I think we're finished here."

The men stood, looked at William, then to his assistant and lastly, to his head of security. The lead consultant started to speak but hesitated momentarily before continuing. "It is our understanding, Mr. Hartman, that you wanted an outside team brought in. I was told that you weren't satisfied with what is going on here in-house. I would ask that you please allow—"

William cut him off and pointed at the door. "As I said, there's nothing more to discuss here."

The men looked to one another, nodded and exited the room. William closed the door behind them. He turned his attention to the men who remained seated and brushed his hands together. "Good riddance."

Paul, his assistant, was the first to speak. "William," he said cautiously. "We need to talk—"

His attorney and longtime friend interrupted, also treading carefully. "We're a bit worried, to tell you the truth. The board has called a meeting. It's about your... situation..."

William scoffed. "*My* situation?"

"They're claiming your behavior lately has been rather... *um*... erratic. They're proposing that you take some time off. Considering..."

"Like fucking hell," William stated, his tone seething. "This is *my* company. I'll be the judge of *if* and *when* I need to take time off." He ran his fingers through his hair and took a deep breath in to calm himself. Finally, he added. "I'm fine."

"William, please," the man pleaded. "Just a week or two... Don't make them force you out. Don't give them a reason. We all know that there are at least a few board members who would kill for the chance... and it won't look good. Please. Take a few weeks off. It'll do you some good..."

William considered his longtime friend, shook his head, and swallowed hard.

Then he opened the door and walked out.

~

As William waited at the door for Sondra to buzz him in, he removed the slip of paper from his suit pocket and unfolded the note.

Dear William,

I think I loved you from the first moment I saw you.

All I knew then

Was all I know now.

I needed more.

72

xx,

YOUR NUMBER ONE FAN

THE WORDS WASHED OVER HIM TAKING HIM BACK TO A different time, a different place.

William stared at the men's size eleven leather shoes. This was a new pair, he was fairly sure. Every day around this time, he had taken to studying the different kinds of shoes his stepfather wore. He felt the cord come down on him once more. He tried not to hold his breath but the plastic burned as it tore through his skin. His stepfather's weapon of choice was the vacuum cleaner cord that afternoon. Two days before, it had been the toaster.

He listened carefully to the man's breathing, this is how he knew how much more to expect, all the while he studied each brown crease in his shoes. He could smell the alcohol on his breath with each inhale and exhale and knew it wouldn't be long now. His stepfather couldn't go on forever. He was winded today, seemingly more intoxicated than the day before, and yet this didn't bode well for William.

Suddenly, he dropped the cord at William's side. "From the first moment I laid eyes on you, I knew you'd amount to nothing. Your own parents evidently don't want you so they left the job to me. Well, you know what that means? It means... I am your father now, and you will do as I say."

"Say something damn it," his stepfather demanded, nudging him with his shoe.

"Yes, sir."

"Good," he said, lighting a cigarette. "Now, we seem to be getting somewhere..." He took a long slow drag and exhaled. "Come to think of it... I want a letter saying as much. Consider this your first contract," he laughed. He took another drag. "Fifteen pages minimum," he added through the smoke. "I want to hear you explain what a decent vacu-uming job actually looks like."

"Yes, sir," William said again.

"Better," his stepfather told him, nodding. He slurred his words as he spoke. William looked on as he took a sip of his whiskey. He kicked William in the ribs once, harder than the last time and he continued, "You'll thank me someday, boy. I want to know that you appreciate what I'm providing for you here. God knows, that whore of a mother you have doesn't." He shook his head and stubbed out the cigarette on William's back. "It's time I started getting more out of the both of you," he told him. *Press. Press. Press. Burn. Burn. Burn.* "You little ungrateful bastard. Why can't you see I need more? Why can't you people understand that?"

This time William didn't answer.

'Because you're bloody stupid," he spat. He looked William over from head to toe. William could feel his eyes on him. Then he followed up with one final blow to William's kneecap. He rolled and winced at the intensity of the pain, rocking back and forth, back and forth. And even though occasionally, to this day, his kneecap still gave him trouble, at the tender age of six, he realized it was the words that would eat at him long after the physical pain had subsided.

The massive door swung open, and all of a sudden, Sondra stood before him bringing the present back into full focus. She took one look at him, shook her head, and stepped aside to allow him in. Once inside the apartment, he made no offer of pleasantries, instead he walked over to the couch where he perched himself on the edge. "We have a problem."

Sondra cocked her head. "Tell me about it."

William gave her a look that was intended to let her know he meant business. He held up the note. "I got another letter today. This *one* was in my office."

"Yeah, so… it's just another secret admirer… you said that. Remember?"

William frowned. "You don't get it. This is different."

"And?"

"And I have a bad feeling about this one. And at any rate— it's not just that. We *have* to find out who this person is… because whoever it is… *they* know."

"They know *what*?" Sondra quizzed. "You've been very paranoid lately…"

"This isn't paranoia," he said, staring at the letter in his hand.

"I hate to say it, William, but have you considered getting a script to help get you through?"

"I don't need medication."

"Maybe just a little something to help you sleep? At the very least, something to take the edge off. Because our meetings don't seem to be doing it for you. Not the way they once did."

William sighed heavily. "You're missing the point entirely. This person… they know we're meeting. They placed the first one on my car. That's *why* I'm *here* this time…"

"You're right," Sondra told him. "I'm not seeing your point…"

William flexed his jaw. "Well, it doesn't look good, these meetings… Also, I've been having more memories."

Sondra narrowed her eyes. "Memories?"

"Flashbacks."

"I'm not surprised…"

"Well, I am. Because it's causing problems."

"Look—"

"No," William said. "You look— it all started with these letters. It's almost like this person knows me. Knows my triggers—"

Sondra crossed her arms, walked over to where he sat,

75

and backhanded him so hard the sound of his teeth hitting one another reverberated inside his ears. "You need to talk to your wife."

He exhaled slowly and rubbed at his jaw.

She cracked her knuckles once and then again, and he flinched a little, knowing what was to come. This time he had just wanted to talk. Mostly. She handed him a mouth guard and ordered him onto his knees. "Put your hands behind your back."

"I want to discuss the letters. I think you can help…"

She shook her head and waited for him to obey. Eventually, he did. "You're pathetic," was all she'd said.

William kneeled and positioned himself in front of her without another word. He took the next blow and the next, all the while staring at the floor. When the last one finally came, he smiled, stood slowly, and thanked her. There wasn't much else to say.

Sondra massaged one wrist and then the other. "I think it's time you take up boxing or mixed martial arts. This is getting a bit ridiculous. And anyhow, I trained your wife for this as I'm sure you can recall."

Mixed martial arts was a good cover, for sure. He knew because he'd already used it. William pursed his lips. "You're right," he agreed. "I need to talk to her. I know I do."

"Then do it. And leave me out of your personal life. As far as finding out who is sending you letters… you need to pull yourself together. There is no *we*, William. Do you understand that?"

"You've made it pretty clear," he said licking blood from his bottom lip.

"Well, good. Let me be more clear—you're a liar and you're cheating on your wife by showing up to see me week after week. You provide funding for my interests and you pay incredibly well, but that's all this is—*we*— as in you and me, we are *not* friends. It would really serve you well to keep that in mind."

"I will," he replied. He used the cuff of his shirt to dab at the blood on his lip. He'd never much cared for the taste of blood. Sondra, it seemed, didn't have the same aversion. He grabbed his coat and headed for the door.

"Oh, and William?"

He slowed slightly.

"I was sorry to hear about the miscarriage."

William deadpanned but he didn't turn to face her.

"Yeah, me, too," he said before slamming the door behind him.

∾

WILLIAM WAS PRACTICALLY MANIC. HE HADN'T SLEPT FOR DAYS, but he'd just had his best idea in quite a while. He rang Addison. She'd hardly had the chance to say hello before he began speaking over her. "We're going back to Capri."

"What?"

"We leave this weekend…" he told her. He spoke hurriedly.

"This weekend? William… I can't leave the country *this* weekend."

"What do you mean you can't leave?"

"I'm already so behind at work as it is…"

"So, let your staff handle it. That's what they're there for."

"I'm still in the process of training my assistant," she told him before she paused. "She's great and all, but you know these things take time…"

"Fine. Bring her with you then. I planned on bringing Paul…"

She sighed. "And the boys? Did you forget that I have children?" He couldn't help but notice the way her voice tripped on the word I. "Anyway," she continued, *"They* have plans. They have soccer games and—"

"So they can come with us, too. Otherwise, let Patrick handle it. He seems to have no problem shifting his responsibilities onto you."

"I can't, William. Not now. I mean... I'm still recovering after—"

William stayed quiet. She'd backed him into a corner knowing there wasn't a rebuttal for that particular excuse.

"Maybe in a few weeks…"

He ran his fingers through his hair and then checked his watch. "All right. Well, we'll see. I've gotta run now though."

"Okay," she'd said sounding relieved. "Listen—I'm sorry it doesn't work for me right now. But we'll get back there soon."

"Yeah," he answered distractedly.

"Oh, and William?"

"Yeah?"

"I love you."

"I love you," he replied.

William ended the call and dialed her office directly.

After getting her assistant on the line, he advised her to clear his wife's schedule, adamant in demanding Addison not be informed of any of it. She agreed, and without a single bit of hesitation. In fact, she seemed delighted when she was asked to come along.

When that was taken care of, he picked up the phone and texted Sondra: I'm taking my wife (i.e. your best employee) out of the country for a week or so. Deal with it.

He read the text back to himself and smiled. *It was too bad she didn't consider him a friend.*

And for a moment, all seemed right in his world again.

～

Addison rested her head against the back of her seat and glared out the small window. Anything to avoid looking over at him. Now that it was done and they were in the air, well on their way, she wanted to let it go. She did. But there was the other part of her, the one who refused to fail, that wanted to fight. She'd let herself go in her first marriage. She'd let so much go that before long, she wasn't sure what she was fighting for any longer. She'd lost her voice, her will to fight and there was a point, a shift, one that had occurred so gradually that, she couldn't pinpoint when and where it happened.

Nonetheless, she'd fought hard to become the woman she was today. The one that the man sitting next to her had fallen in love with and married. And, no matter how controlling, no matter how wealthy, or how handsome, or how much she loved him, she wouldn't let him destroy that.

Clearly, there was a breakdown occurring and it was up to her to set things straight. Only he wasn't making it easy over there with his faded jeans, white t-shirt, tussled hair, and classic devil-may-care attitude. Had they been alone, she would have climbed over onto his lap and fixed the situation, she would have made it right, then and there. But true to his nature, he'd insisted on bringing both their assistants along for the ride. This was something she wasn't sure she'd ever get used to, the complete and utter lack of privacy. She couldn't even have a proper fight with her husband without half a dozen of their staff being caught up in the mix.

William stood and grabbed her wrist. "I need to speak with you."

She raised her brow and looked from side to side. *A challenge.* An unspoken question. He was good at reading her, she'd give him that.

"Now," he said nodding toward the back of the plane.

Addison gave him a look and then stood and followed him down the aisle.

Behind the divider, he placed his hand on her hip and slid the door shut. He lowered his voice and took her chin in his hands. "This has to stop," he said searching her eyes. "I know you didn't want to come along on this trip. But here we are."

"Here we are," she said, glancing away.

"I need this, Addison. I need *you*."

She pulled back. "Yeah, well, I need you to listen when I say no."

"I don't see what the big deal is," William sighed. "I rearranged the boys' games. I fixed the issue at work. I don't understand why getting my wife alone should be so hard—"

"Paying off soccer teams seems a little excessive," she replied, shaking her head. "Rearranging my schedule without my permission is just plain bullshit."

He pushed her against the wall, and slid his palms up the back of her thighs. "You're beautiful when you're angry… you know that?"

"William." She sighed.

He smiled. "And to be fair, I didn't pay off a soccer team. I simply compensated them for a little bit of rearranging on their part. As for your schedule, well…"

"You—"

He cut her off by leaning into her. He kissed her mouth and then went in for the kill, trailing his mouth down, down, down. And while she wanted to argue, her body gave in to his touch. It gave her away, she wasn't as strong as she thought she was and they both knew it. Suddenly, she found herself in a position where she agreed without words.

"What do you say we settle this the old fashioned way?" he suggested as he pushed her blouse lower on her chest allowing his mouth to follow.

"I—"

"Come on," he pleaded, the weight of him pushing her further against the wall.

"Here? *Now?*" she asked breathlessly.

He backed off, looked around the small space and then back at her. "Where else?"

She eyed him reverently and then shrugged.

"But that's not what I meant…" he added. "I meant, is it okay… with the doc?"

She sucked in her bottom lip and then undid the top button of his jeans, giving him the answer.

He smiled, leaned in, and covered her mouth with his. "I want to try again," he said, his breath hot on hers.

And while Addison wasn't quite sure exactly what he'd meant by those words, it mattered little in that moment. She simply placed her arms around his neck, leaned in, and buried her face into his chest.

William waited briefly for a response, and when none came, he pulled back slightly, raised her chin, and then lifted her hips to meet his. With one hand, he took both her wrists in his hand and held them in place above her head, making it nearly impossible for her to move.

He adjusted himself and pushed into her slowly, his eyes on hers. He pinned her back against the wall as hard as he could and thrust into her again, just a little harder each time. When he knew she was close, he released her hands and cupped his hand around her throat holding her in position, just the way she liked. "Look at me," he demanded. So she did.

He moved faster then, and when she couldn't keep the moans from escaping her lips, he released her throat and placed his hand over her mouth. Addison held her breath and tried to contain the pleasure that was building in her throat. Another small pleading moan managed to escape. He smiled, and pushed into her harder.

A knock at the door caused William to freeze in place momentarily. Addison's eyes grew wide. She'd already begun her descent into ecstasy and couldn't stop it now.

Another knock. This one more urgent.

He didn't seem to mind the interruption. He simply clasped his palm around her mouth tighter, pulled back slowly, inch by inch, and just when she thought he'd quit, he thrust into her again. *Leave it to William to control even this.*

"One moment," he managed to choke out once he'd finished inside her.

"Mr. Hartman, we need you to return to your seat," the attendant's voice urged. "We're making an emergency landing."

~

CHAPTER TEN

7:25 AM

My dearest William,

I want to apologize that my little situation caused you added stress and expense. But if I'm being honest, and well, you know how I feel about that... personally, I've always found it to be kind of a double-edged sword.

Here's what happened:

I saw the way you looked at her, and it didn't sit well with me. Do you have any idea how hard I worked to get you to notice me? And yet, nothing. Nada. Zip. Zilch. Not a single glance.

Needless to say, it didn't take long for me to realize that I was pretty much invisible to you.

To make matters worse, I hadn't eaten in four days. FOUR DAYS, WILLIAM. Nothing but water and okay, sure, a bite of lettuce here or there. But only when I had to take my meds. Needless to say, I was on top of my game. I looked better than ever!

I'd worked hard to look as good as your wife did. Not all of us are blessed with good genetics, you know.

But I digress.

Because you didn't even fucking notice. And I would be damned if my starvation, dehydration, and hearty usage of laxatives would be in vain. You have no idea how many hours upon hours I spent sitting on the shitter, my stomach cramping while I plotted and planned. I wanted to tell Addison that I understood what a miscarriage must feel like, at least physically. But thought better of it. I still need my job. For now.

Anyhow, I did everything you asked and—even a few things you didn't.

It was ME who finally had the joy of telling your wife about the trip. It was *me* who listened to her rant and rave about it—about your incessant need for control. She was completely and annoyingly irate over the whole thing. She has no idea how lucky she is.

Meanwhile, my panties were wet.

You and I, William, we are one of a kind.

We take what we want, and we do it by taking matters into our own hands.

So when I saw that you had no interest in taking notice of me, that's exactly what I did.

I was sure you'd understand.

I did exactly as you did.

After all, it was your bloody fault we were on this trip to begin with.

You want me.

I know it.

So stop playing hard to get.

It's only making things more difficult.

For the others.

Love always,

L

P.S. A poem just for you:

Word Play.

You tell me what I want to hear.

Like any skilled seductor,

you play me like a fiddle—

strumming to the tune of your choosing.

Only I see right through you—

I love you anyway.

And so, I let you play.

For the music is just too good

84

to make it stop.

~

2:14 PM

Dear William,

I wrote you something else so that perhaps you will understand me a bit better.

The Opposite of Half-Ass.

All I ever wanted

from the beginning

was to love you

in the only way

I knew how.

Which, unfortunately

for us both was

all the way.

I am not a half-ass kind of person, William. I am not.

And, while many people would look at the things I've done and judge them as bad, it's only because most people are unable to see both sides of the coin.

Most people, William, see what they want to see.

But not you.

And certainly not me.

I wanted your attention.

And I got it.

I apologize about poor Paul. He wasn't my intended victim, but sometimes, that's just the way it works out, unfortunately.

By now, you probably know that I like to pick up men.

But I want to tell you the *how* and the *why* of it.

When I was in college, I was a shy girl. It's a shame but basically life circumstances led me to be meek. Very unlike I am today. You see, love, and I know you of all people get this, there comes a point in life where you have to decide whether you want to be a shark or simply one of those pretty fish that swim with the pack. Up until that point in my life, I liked being a part of the pack. I wanted to be one of them. Mostly because there is safety in numbers. I wanted to fit in. Merely fitting in only takes one so far, though. And lo' and behold if the motherfucking sharks didn't single me out.

They pushed me, William.

And I bet they did the same to you.

I didn't have a lot of friends my freshman year of college. What I did have was a room-mate. And she had friends so I liked to pretend. One night, to my surprise, they invited me out with them. I didn't really like loud music or clubs, but I thought, what the hell. "I bet she's never even been drunk," I heard one of them say. "Yeah, well, look at her. I bet she's still a virgin," the other said.

But my roommate, Sarah, she wasn't really like the rest of them. Or so I thought. She was kind and very, very pretty. She dressed me up, fixed my hair, and made me look like... well... *her.*

So we go to this club, and I'm determined, William. I am determined to show them. I will prove that I *am* like them. That I am a girl who can hold her liquor. That I am not *still a virgin,* even though I was.

After a few rounds of shots, Sarah said some of her guy friends wanted to meet up with us at another club, and so we left. This is rule number one of how bad things happen, William. Never let them take you to a second location. I learned that then.

At the second club, there were more rounds of shots and most importantly... cute boys. And they were paying attention to me, William. So much attention. One of them even asked Sarah where she'd been hiding me all this time.

Speaking of my roommate, that guy and I, well, we got to talking about her and he tells me they used to date and how I remind him of Sarah. This was nice, but I knew I could never go out with a friend's ex—that would be wrong, and so I mostly turned my atten-tion elsewhere. Only he didn't stop there. He upped his game. And to tell you the truth, I kind of liked it. I appreciated a man who knew what he wanted and went for it. He bought me drinks, and later, he pulled me out onto the dance floor. I'd never danced with a boy before. I was spinning, the room was spinning, my whole world was spinning—and for the first time ever, I felt really alive.

At some point while we were out on the dance floor, my so-called friends decided it was time to leave. I vaguely remember Sarah telling me that I should go with them, although I

86

must have resisted a bit, and while she looked concerned, or maybe it was sad, she didn't push.

That was one of her first mistakes, William. She should have pushed.

For the next six hours, I went in and out of consciousness as approximately seven (or so I counted) fraternity brothers took turns with me. I awoke later that morning naked on a filthy couch in a basement, my body bloody and bruised, my hair matted together by their bodily fluids, my skin covered in urine. They say you're not supposed to remember these things when you're drugged, William, but I remembered more than I ever wanted to. I remember the way they laughed and joked as they had their way with me. I remember how, for a while, I tried to fight, and I remember at which point I finally gave up. They'd said I wanted it, as they spat on my naked body, but they were wrong. They were sharks, and I was their prey. Merely a fish out of water. Left behind by the pack.

But, hey, at least I wasn't a virgin any longer, right?

Sarah must have known what had happened when I didn't come home that night and also, I'm guessing by the bruises on my body. I made sure not to cover them whenever I changed. But she never said anything.

And that was her second mistake.

For I'd learned what it meant to be a shark.

So much love,

L

$\sim$

4:24 PM

Dear William,

You're probably wondering why I just told you all of that, so let me explain.

That was how I first got my start with 'Roofies.' Rohypnol. That's the date rape drug, in case you aren't aware.

And it was the beginning of me becoming a shark—learning to take what I wanted in life or else be taken from.

You know what they say, 'swim with the fishes or get eaten by the sharks.'

Well, fuck that, William. I no longer wanted to swim with anyone. I wanted to be a shark.

So I learned to pick up spineless little weasels like Sarah's ex-boyfriend. I started with the original seven, and I gave each of them a taste of their own medicine. I hurt them, William. I hurt them bad.

But I won't spill all my secrets as to how here in this letter. After all, a little mystery is good for a relationship. Don't you think?

Anyway, the 'Roofie' that caused the emergency landing wasn't intended for Paul at all. He was an innocent bystander, and if I have to say so myself, an idiot who can't keep track of his own drink. Or maybe he's one of those weirdos who likes to drink other people's drinks. In that case, he got what was coming to him. And really, you'd be amazed at all of the weird shit I've seen people do.

As for me, I was too busy trying to listen to you and your wife going at it to notice exactly what happened with the whole drink situation. I was rubbing one out in the bathroom and thinking of you when the attendant knocked to tell me to get back to my seat, that we were preparing for landing. When I emerged, I could clearly see that it was Paul who'd consumed the drink I'd mixed up especially for your wife.

I didn't want to hurt her.

Really I didn't.

I just wanted to knock her out of the game for a bit so I could advance.

But sometimes, even the best-laid plans have unintended consequences.

In this case, Paul suffered.

I gained.

He really shouldn't have been a fish.

More on that later...

Love you lots,

L

—STILL YOUR NUMBER ONE FAN

〜

CHAPTER ELEVEN

William and Addison spent eight hours grounded in Chicago while they awaited the news of what might be causing Paul's slurred speech and extreme drowsiness. After five hours in the ER, it turned out that no significant health condition was found—nothing obvious could explain the symptoms he presented.

William insisted on putting him on a plane homeward bound while Paul insisted he was fine to continue on with the trip.

In the end, they agreed to layover until morning, and by six AM the following day, Paul seemed back to his usual self.

A few hours into the flight, William and Paul were working on a proposal when Paul leaned in close. "There's something about that woman I don't like."

William cocked his head. "And that would be?"

Paul considered the question and then let out a short sigh. "I can't pinpoint it exactly," he admitted. "But give me time..."

William glanced over at his wife then. She was immersed in the conversation she was having with her assistant, and whatever the two were discussing, it seemed to hold her attention. He raised his brow. "Well, my wife seems to really like her."

"That's the thing," Paul said. "She looks like Addison, kind of, you know?"

William narrowed his gaze and studied the women.

"But it's like she's working at it," Paul added. "Does that make sense?"

William studied the woman more carefully. He hadn't really noticed before, but something about her did seem familiar.

Paul shifted. "And she said the strangest thing to me yesterday..."

"Which was?"

"She said that we were on the same team so I should start acting like it."

William laughed. "Well, you just said yourself you don't like her."

"Yeah... and I think you need to keep an eye on her," Paul warned. "She just seems—I don't know... a bit off."

William smirked. "Aren't they all?"

⌁

THAT NIGHT, THE FOUR OF THEM HAD DINNER ON A PRIVATE balcony overlooking the ocean. The sky turned a brilliant shade of red against the backdrop of the setting sun. "This view is breathtaking," Lydia remarked.

William leaned in close and whispered in his wife's ear. "Thank you for coming."

Addison smiled. "The pleasure's all mine."

Lydia winced so hard the table shook. All eyes turned to her. "I'm sorry," she said. "I think something bit me..."

"That'll happen here," William assured her.

"Addison says you have a house here."

"Yes, but we're doing some renovations, and I figured we'd be more comfortable here."

Lydia smiled. The fact that he'd said 'we' wasn't lost on her.

The conversation flowed, and once a few more drinks had been consumed, Paul stopped seemingly mid-bite, laid his fork on his plate, and turned his attention directly to Lydia. "So...," he said pausing to glance at William before continuing. "I really don't know much about you..."

She laughed nervously. "Well, there's not really much to know."

Paul furrowed his brow. "Ah," he said. "I'm sure that's not true. Why don't you tell us about yourself?"

Lydia seemed to light up under his complement. Then just as quickly her expression shifted. "Seriously..." she reiterated. "There's not really much to tell."

He glanced down at her ring finger. "You're not married?"

"No."

"Boyfriend?"

"No," she blushed. "Not really."

"How about kids?"

Lydia deadpanned. She clenched her hands into fists. Her jaw set and then she recovered. "Someday."

"Hmmm," Paul replied, pressing his lips together. "Well, I guess you weren't joking then—you really *don't* have a lot going on."

"Paul," William warned.

"Ah, it's okay, Mr. Hartman. I don't mind. And really, you're right, Paul," Lydia remarked. "Right now, my main focus in life is my work. It's what brings me the greatest satisfaction. I figure there's plenty of time to worry about becoming domesticated."

"That's understandable," William said before he glanced

over at Paul, clearly offering another warning. "And Mr. Hartman was my father. Call me William. Please."

Addison cocked her head to the side, studied her husband's profile, and then turned her attention to the waves crashing against the shore. The wine had finally hit her, and she found herself somewhere far off, away from the table, away from dinner. She found herself reflecting back on their first time here.

"There's probably less time than you think..." Paul uttered bringing Addison back to the present.

Lydia smiled and looked to William. "We'll see," she said, raising her brow. "Like I said—right now, I'm just focused on where I'm at."

"That's not a bad place to focus," Addison chimed. She glanced over at her husband and then back out over the ocean. She raised her glass of wine. "To us," she toasted.

"To us," they repeated in unison, glasses raised.

And if there had been any doubt in Lydia's mind before about this being meant to be—it dissolved in that moment.

Just like that, she realized she had officially gained her ticket in.

&

ADDISON WATCHED WILLIAM STEP INSIDE, LOOK FROM SIDE TO side, and finally close the door behind him. "So you're saying you don't think it's a bit odd that she followed us all the way back to our room?"

She exhaled as she kicked off her heels. "She's a lot to take... I get it. But if you could see how much she's already accomplished for me. She really knows her stuff. I mean... if I ask for something... she doesn't just deliver. She knocks it out of the park. She really goes well above and beyond. And I've never had an assistant quite like that."

William raised his brow. "She seems... pretty into you."

"Overbearing you mean?"

He swallowed. "You could say that."

She took the keycard from his hand. "I think she just wants to be my friend."

He crossed his arms and leaned against the wall. "Be careful there."

Addison cocked her head to the side. "I am," she replied defiantly, tossing the room card on the table in the entryway. She turned and motioned for him to unzip her zipper. "Anyway, enough about her. There's something I need to talk to you about..."

"Hmmm. Well, I had something else in mind," he told her, studying the small of her back.

She smiled, turned to face him, and stepped out of her dress. "I'm sure you did."

He ran his hands down the length of her arms, stepped backward, and eyed her black lace bra and matching panties. "Talking," he said. "Just seems overrated when your wife looks like this."

Addison sighed, smiled and took him by the hand. "Oh, yeah?" she asked, leading him over to the sofa. She gently pushed him down onto it.

"Yeah," he said eyeing her patiently. He parted his legs and motioned for her to step in between them. He leaned forward, inhaled her scent, and placed his face against her stomach. The stubble on his face tickled and she laughed. William looked up at her with an expression that let her know he wasn't messing around. He took her wrists into one hand and held them behind her back.

He kissed her stomach, trailing his lips down to the edge of her panties where he stopped abruptly. "Actually, you're right. We do need to talk," he whispered against her belly.

"Seriously?" she sighed heavily. "I had other things in

mind," she confessed, running her fingers through his hair, directing his head south where she desperately wanted his mouth to go.

"I figured," he said, glancing up. He peeled her underwear off and then he parted her legs, letting his mouth linger as he gave her what she wanted. Finally, when her knees grew too weak to stand, he pulled her onto his lap. As she straddled him, he watched her body glide up and down, the two of them nothing more than shadows dancing in the moonlight, consumed by what they craved.

And thankfully, for the both of them, few words were required.

~

THE NEXT MORNING, ADDISON AWOKE TO THE AROMA OF coffee and bacon, and the sound of laughter coming from the living room.

She propped herself up, reached over, and checked the time on her phone. *It was still so early.*

Exhausted, she sank back down into the tangled mess of sheets and closed her eyes. She attempted to listen for the waves crashing against the shore, but it was Lydia's voice that she heard filling the air.

She rolled over onto her side and checked her phone once more, scanning her email. There were thirteen from her assistant alone. And now here she was. *Had she even slept? Did she ever sleep?*

The thing about Lydia was that she caused Addison to have to up her game. She was helpful, no doubt. But she also caused Addison to have to work harder. Lydia was hungry, full of energy and excitement, and clearly had a love of winning. *All things that came with being new.* It would slow down soon enough, Addison realized. But for now, she was giving into it, she was riding the wave. They'd closed more new accounts in the last month than they had in all of the previous quarter, and this was considering that a portion of the time she'd been out recovering from the miscarriage.

The truth was, Addison longed for the days when she'd still had that hunger. She listened to Lydia's words last night about becoming 'domesticated' and she wondered if that was what was happening with her all over again.

She brushed the thought aside and inhaled the salty warm air before typing out replies to a few of the emails. Then she thought better of letting Lydia know she was awake. She wanted time alone with her husband and so she placed them in her draft folder and laid her phone on the bedside table. Eventually, she heard the front door close. Seconds later, William appeared in the doorway carrying a plate of food. Shirtless and smiling, the dark circles under his eyes were telltale signs that he hadn't slept either. *He hadn't been sleeping much these days, it seemed.*

Addison eyed him from head to toe stopping at the place where his pajama bottoms hung low on his hips. She raised her brow. "You're up early."

He took a bite of bacon, walked over, and perched himself on the bed beside her. "Yeah," he remarked. "Your assistant thought we needed breakfast."

Addison picked up a slice of bacon, sniffed it, and then placed it back on the plate. "Well, that was nice of her."

He eyed her, his mouth twisted.

She frowned. "What?"

He seemed to contemplate what to say before settling on his response. "Nothing."

She turned over onto her stomach and inched closer to him. "That look didn't say *nothing*."

He looked away then, out at the water. "Hey," he said,

eventually. "I was thinking we should get out of here today. Get away... just the two of us."

"Okay."

William leaned forward and playfully slapped her bottom. "That sort of requires you getting up."

Addison inhaled and then slowly exhaled. *It was now or never.* "Okay," she said. But first, I need to tell you something..."

He looked down at her and waited.

"I don't think I want to have another baby."

"What?"

"I went back on the pill."

He stiffened, and his expression changed instantly to one of confusion. "What do you mean?" He shook his head. "Ever?"

"I don't know—I... just don't think I can do it again."

"That doesn't make any sense..." he said. "You were so happy to be pregnant."

"I know."

"Then what changed?"

"Well, for one, I'm not pregnant anymore."

William winced. "So, you're saying *never*? You really don't want any more kids?"

Addison shook her head and then she shrugged. "I don't know."

He sighed, and she'd wanted to say more but she wondered if there was really anything left she *could* say. She realized this was going to be a blow he wasn't prepared for.

Eventually, he stood, walked to the door, stopping just inside the doorframe. "You've been through a lot," he told her. "You'll change your mind..."

"I'm not so sure," she finally said.

But it was too late.

He'd already turned to go.

BEYOND BEDROCK

CHAPTER TWELVE

Addison checked her appearance in the mirror once more before gathering her things. *He would like these shorts.* She needed him to like them. *She'd done it. Finally.* She told him. And now the tiniest part of her regretted it. *He was hurt.* She'd known he would be. *And what if he was right? What if she changed her mind? Maybe she shouldn't have said anything at all.* Maybe everything in a marriage didn't need to be said.

She dug through her bag in search of her mascara and pulled out lip-gloss instead. Her phone chimed. She placed the lip-gloss on the counter, dug into the bag, pulled her phone out, and checked it. Two new texts from Lydia, one from her son, and one from a number she didn't recognize. She checked the text from Parker but left the others. Then she touched up her makeup, only to pick the phone up again when it chimed.

"Let's go," William called down the hall. "Boats don't wait."

"I'm coming," she assured him as her eyes glossed over the texts.

Addison clicked on one of the messages from Lydia about

work and then replied to her son. Awaiting his response, she clicked on the text from the unknown number. An image popped up. It was a photo of William coming out of a high-rise building. Below the photo read: YOUR HUSBAND IS A DIRTY LIAR.

Addison's heart raced as she studied the photo more carefully. She knew that building well. *It was Sondra's building.*

She walked into the living room to find her husband sitting at the bar, dressed in khaki shorts and a gray t-shirt. She hadn't remembered the last time he'd looked so laid back, this carefree. "So," she said, keeping her tone neutral. "When are we going to talk about the fact that you haven't been sleeping..."

He ignored her question and instead eyed her up and down. A smile crept over his features. "Come here and let me see those shorts."

Addison didn't come there. She folded her arms. She didn't budge. "We need to talk."

He hated those words. She knew it.

He tilted his head. "So talk."

"Any idea what this is about?" she asked handing him the phone.

William studied the screen and then ran his fingers through his hair. After a few seconds he stood and walked to the couch. He took a deep breath and dropped down onto it. She followed. But she didn't sit. She waited.

"Yes," he finally answered.

Addison sighed. "And?"

He looked down at the floor and then back at her.

She stood over him. "Why were you at Sondra's apartment? Why would someone send me this?"

He twisted his mouth. "I don't know."

"More importantly," she scoffed. "*Who* would send this?"

"I—" A knock at the door interrupted them.

William looked to the door, then back at her, and stood slowly.

She cleared her throat and grabbed his forearm. "William?"

"I've—" he started to say but was cut off by another knock.

He looked her in the eye and sighed. "Give me a sec…" he said, holding up his hands, removing his arm from her grip. "Let me make whoever this is go away," he added. "And then I'll explain everything…"

Addison sighed. She hesitated briefly before she stepped aside and let him pass. She watched him walk toward the door and her heart sank. It was always going to be this way with him. A life of constant interruptions.

William opened the door to find two uniformed officers standing outside. He raised his brow. "Are you William Hartman?" The shorter of the two was the first to speak.

He cocked his head to the side and didn't answer right away, putting the ball in their court. "Yes," he answered finally. "That's me."

This time the taller man took the lead. "Paul Mayfield's room is listed in your name," he said. "Are the two of you related?"

William shook his head. "He's my assistant."

The taller officer peered over his head and then looked him directly in the eye. "May we come in?"

He studied their faces for a moment before stepping aside and motioning them in. William had just begun to close the door when the shrill of her voice stopped him. "Mr. Hartman! Oh, my God. Mr. Hartman!"

He turned back and reopened the door, just a little to find Lydia standing opposite him. She was panting, completely out of breath. Her eyes wild. "I am so sorry. *So sorry*," she exclaimed. William searched her eyes. "I know how much Paul meant to you."

He turned to face the officers standing in his entryway and then looked back at Lydia.

"What is going on?" he demanded.

Lydia threw herself into his arms. "It's Paul," she cried. "Paul is dead."

5:56 AM

Dearest William,

I admit it… I kind of lost it after your wife texted me to say you guys were going off island for the day. Arguably, it could be said that I'd lost it the night before when I expected you to invite me in for a nightcap. But you didn't. I did everything right, and all I wanted was a little more time, and you refused me.

You have all that success, William, and zero manners. Who would've thought? Apparently, not I.

At any rate, I settled for the next best thing. I went to your assistant. I went to his room, and I told him your wife had asked that I work with him on some scheduling stuff, and lo and behold, he bought it! Well, not really, I don't think. I'm pretty sure he saw right through me. But I think he must have wanted to get a closer look at what I might be up to and so he totally let me in.

His mistake.

That's always their mistake, my dear William. Their intuition says don't. Don't do it. Something isn't right. But curiosity wins out. Every. Single. Time. Curiosity or their dick —who's to say?

Anyhow, we spent a few minutes working, and then I offered him a drink. I have a million costumes, and that night, I donned my shy, dumb, and sexy one. I also wore white. For purity. But you knew that.

I pretended to be that girl I was back in college, and I was amazing at it. I seduced him like nobody's business. I started out playing hard to get. But not that hard. And once Paul sensed he might have a way in—like the rest of them—he took it.

That's the thing about men, William. If they believe there's even the slightest chance that it might be easy, they're all over it. I never met a man who said no. Not a one. Well, that is, until you.

Unfortunately for Paul, his first mistake was letting me in. His second was trying to sleep with me. His final was making us drinks. There's nothing worse than a man so unconfident in his abilities that he has to use alcohol to further his agenda. Whatever happened to good old-fashioned romance anyway?

I know without a doubt that you're not like Paul. You're different than the rest of them. That's why we're in this mess, William.

One drink in, and you know what? He never did ask about those scheduling issues I'd mentioned. Another mistake on his part. It proved he wasn't hardcore. He was just a pussy who wanted mine. But he knew little in the way of seduction. Paul also probably didn't know that a certain well-touted sleeping aid could be lethal. A little too much and *voila*, your little sleep problem just became permanent. It took three drinks, love. THREE. Usually, I settle matters by the second, but Paul was admittedly a bit trickier than the others were. He didn't really like turning his back on me. I could tell. He had doubts about me, and it showed. He had reservations about what we were doing. Albeit, clearly, not enough to save his life.

The thing was, William, Paul didn't like me. Worst of all, he was terrible at hiding it. But he liked my pussy, that's for sure. I hate to say it. I hate to tell you that I let it go that far. But it did.

You chose your wife that night. And I chose Paul.

You should have seen the look on his face as I rode his cock. I don't think he thought I had it in me. Trouble is, the thing I hate more than anything is to be underestimated. I put it down on him, William. Eventually, the drugs started to kick in, and I could tell he suspected something was wrong—in fact—*he knew.* I could see it in his eyes.

There's no greater aphrodisiac in this world than knowing you have the upper hand, William.

Surely, you know this.

Paul liked what I gave him.

And while he did ask for help once or twice, mostly in the form of water—never once did he ask me to stop. He let me keep going… all the while, he slowly drifted off to Never-Never Land. Not a bad way to die if you think about it, actually.

And you should.

Hell, we all should.

Later, after I'd gotten mine—a few times—and once he was out cold, I carefully placed the remainder of the pills in a few key places. Two on his nightstand. Three in his suit pocket. And a handful tucked away in his luggage. Truth is, I always hate to let good drugs go to waste—but what's a girl to do?

Once that was taken care of, I slid his briefs up and threw his legs over the side of the bed. Turns out, he was a tighty-whitey kind of guy, which I hate—but I probably should've guessed. You tell by how uptight a person is.

Paul was an addict, he couldn't say no. Maybe not to drugs, but definitely to drinks and sex. Now, he just so happened to look like one. He got what was coming to him. Even if he wouldn't have taken those pills knowingly, he craved what I dished out. He wanted an escape and that's what I gave him.

It didn't have to be that way, really it didn't. He shouldn't have filled your head with lies about me, love. This was his fault. You were with her, and I was with him. If he hadn't made me look stupid, it might have been different. He should have treated me better. Otherwise, he should have said no. At least then, maybe I could have respected him. Who knows, maybe he could have even lived. After all, I know how hard good assistants are to find...

Anyway, it was these things I pondered as I waited for him to stop breathing. Thankfully, and you will be happy to know that it didn't take long. Once they start foaming at the mouth, you know your time is almost up and you can go—that you can get back to business. Waiting for a person to die can be hell, my love. Sometimes you have to help them along. But usually not. Personally, though, I put my time to good use while I waited by working. Mostly, I emailed your wife.

Finally, when he looked dead enough, after I'd checked for a pulse and found none, I headed back to my room and ordered your breakfast. For a moment, I considered slipping your wife a little something easy (nothing harsh like Paul. I'm aware of my dosages, no worries!) but I was afraid you might ingest it by mistake, and God knows I couldn't go the day without seeing your face.

The truth is, I wanted to be there for you when you found out about Paul.

And you almost robbed me of that, William.

All because you wanted to get away. With her.

But I couldn't let you.

So I caused a bit more trouble.

I know what you're thinking—*as if Paul wasn't enough.*

And I was sorry to have to do that.

I'll make it up to you.

Promise.

Yours forever (and ever),

L

P.S. A poem for you:

Safe Word.

Let me love you

Was all I ever wanted to say,

But I bit my tongue—

Sometimes until it bled.

How little did you know?

That all it would have taken

Was one simple word

From you.

The inkling that it was okay—

That it was safe to let you in.

I would've let you swallow me whole.

And I would've loved every minute.

CHAPTER THIRTEEN

Once the police finally cleared out, and travel arrangements had been made to get them back home, William had intended to tell his wife the truth. He really had. Only his assistant was dead, *her* assistant had ended up staying over in the guest room, and Addison was exhausted. Somehow, it didn't quite feel like the appropriate time to bring up the fact that not only was he being stalked—but also that Sondra had resumed her role as his Dominatrix and he'd been lying to her about it for months.

So, he let it go for the time being. And while neither of them slept that night, neither of them brought it up either.

In fact, neither of them spoke much at all until the following morning when they boarded the plane and his attorney phoned. "I want to give you the heads up that Mr. Mayfield's widow has decided to pursue legal action," he said, a little too grimly for William's liking.

"Hmm," was the best he could muster in response.

His attorney continued, "I'm reaching out because I'd like to discuss the best way to respond. It's important I understand the facts so I know which angle to pursue with her counsel."

William pinched the bridge of his nose between his thumb and forefinger. "Paul hasn't even been dead for twenty-four hours. Is this something we actually *have* to discuss right this very second?"

"She's going to the media, William."

He exhaled loudly. "Wonderful."

"She is claiming that she spoke with her husband following a hospital visit in Chicago, and that he asserted he'd wanted to return home, but he feared for his job if he did so... She's also asserting that her husband informed her you were advised to take a leave of absence due to growing concerns over your erratic behavior. Let's just say she knows a lot of... well... a lot of insider information."

"Great."

"It's quite the opposite actually," his attorney said.

William looked over at his wife and then away. "And?"

His attorney lowered his voice. "And it could be bad if they publicize it, particularly if they claim your judgment was off."

"It wasn't off. It wasn't my call. The physicians will verify that."

"Still—" he replied. "I know you don't need this right now... but I'm afraid this won't look good. Regardless of whether or not it's true. The media will eat this up... like those sweat shop stories. You know how they love a good victim. We can't have that. Especially not with where we are on the Gleason merger. We need to have a plan of counter-attack in motion should she go through with it."

William shifted in his seat to face his wife, who was already working hard to gauge the situation. "The facts are... Paul got sick on the way here. He wanted to continue on—in fact, he insisted— and I didn't resist. As far as what he told his wife about it—I have no idea. We never discussed his personal life. I reached out to her personally last night to offer my condolences, and to let her know everything as far as having his body transported back could be handled by my staff, and that I would take care of funeral expenses. When she asked about future earnings, I said I'd have a human resources manager contact her first thing this morning, and I set that in motion..."

"Good deal," the attorney remarked before pausing. "All right...well, I'll reach out to her counsel, and I'll be in touch soon."

William ended the call and tossed his phone onto the seat opposite him.

"What now?" Addison asked searching his face for answers.

"It sounds like another lawsuit is on the way," he replied matter of factly.

She exhaled and then sunk back into her seat and closed her eyes. "Nice."

"That's not right," Lydia interjected. "You had nothing to do with Paul's death!"

Surprised by the harshness in her tone, William shifted in his seat to face her. He waved her off. "Ah, well," he shrugged. "That's just a part of doing business. It happens."

"Pretty often in your case," Addison added, a definite edge to her voice.

"Well, I still don't think it's right," Lydia said.

He smirked and turned to his wife, who appeared to be trying to doze off. "That's for the court to decide, unfortunately," he eventually added, glancing back over his shoulder.

Lydia cocked her head to the side as she considered his sentiment. "Only if you let it get that far," she finally said.

William laughed. "That's true," he agreed and then he paused briefly, "You remind me of someone..."

Lydia smiled.

Addison shifted and opened her eyes slowly, looking over at her husband. "Would that be Sondra?"

He furrowed his brow. "I really hadn't thought about it."

Addison glared at him for a moment and then stood. "Well, maybe you should," she snapped. Then she turned, walked to the rear of the plane, sliding the door shut behind her.

"She's tired," Lydia remarked staring at the door.

William sighed. "I know."

~

TRAFFIC WAS AT A STANDSTILL, NOTHING BUT A SEA OF RED taillights against a backdrop of gray rain clouds. Heavy Rain pounded the pavement, and it was a lonely kind of rain. The kind that swept you up in it and made you actually believe it was possible that you might never see the sun again. The low hum of the windshield wipers was beginning to drive Addison crazy, and she had gotten to the point that if she didn't get out of that car soon, she feared she might just open the door and flee into the night. She longed to be somewhere else, anywhere else. She wanted to get swept up in the rain— to let it soak her clothes and cleanse her body. Neither of them wanted to be the first to speak, and things inside the car were also at a standstill, not so unlike what was going on outside.

Eventually, when the silence between the two of them had reached a maddening level, William decided he couldn't take it anymore. "Addison..."

She deadpanned at the sound of her name. She'd known it was coming. She just hated the way it sounded in this context. She looked over at him and crossed her arms, taking aim. "When *were* you going to tell me you were seeing her again?"

It seemed as though he'd inhaled all the air around them and exhaled before he finally spoke. "I know," he said. "You're right. I should have told you and... I'm sorry."

"You're sorry?" Her voice hardened. She hated him for saying she was right. For trying to take the edge off, for not giving her the right to be angry. "No," she said, shaking her head. "Sorry, that's all you've got?" she demanded throwing her hands up. "You're sorry. You know what? *That's bullshit.* Come on... why don't you try again. I'm pretty sure you can do better than that—"

"Addison, don't." He turned to look at her then. "Please," he offered, a one-word plea for peace. "Just let me—"

"Let you what? Keep lying? Keep avoiding the fact that there's clearly a problem?"

His jaw hardened. "I was handling it."

She did a double take. "Clearly..." she said shifting in her seat. Then, after a long pause, she added, "What I don't get is... why *her*? Why didn't you come to me?"

He sighed and considered her question. "I don't know."

"Of course you do! Seriously," she replied glaring out the passenger window. "Do you *really* expect me to buy your BS? I know you...William. You don't do anything without careful thought."

He slowed, pulled the car over, and put it in park. He shifted in his seat and put his hand on hers. She pulled away but didn't take her eyes off his. "Look..." he said, softening his tone. "The nightmares came back... and I didn't know what to do... I wasn't sleeping and I didn't want it to get bad like before... and then all of a sudden, it was worse, and seeing Sondra just seemed like the quickest fix."

She swallowed. "That's where you're wrong. Sondra didn't 'fix' you. Falling in love did."

He averted his eyes and stared past her out the window. "Maybe," he admitted. "But you haven't seen me at my worst, Addison. There were times where I could barely get out of bed. There have been days lately where doing so has taken every bit of energy I could muster. Most of the time, I can't eat—and when I can, it hardly stays down. My flashbacks are at an all-time high. Hell, they're trying to force me out of my own company. And I wanted to protect you and the boys from seeing that happen. Seeing Sondra helps. Even if you think it's wrong—and I *knew* you would… I couldn't help it. I refuse to let my past determine my future. I refuse to allow what happened cause me to lose everything. You don't deserve that kind of man…"

"No," she scoffed. "What I don't deserve is a liar."

William winced. "I know," he said before clearing his throat. "But at the same time… this is what you were trained to do. You know exactly why men seek out Dommes—so… I'm not really sure what kind of explanation or clarification you're looking for…"

"Don't patronize me."

"I'm not," he said. "You wanted honesty…"

"Yeah—well, *now*, I don't know what I want."

"You mean, like another child? While we're on the subject of honesty—let's talk about that…"

Addison raised her voice. "What is that supposed to mean?"

"Well, for one, you can't marry a man and then spring it on them that you no longer want to have children with him."

"Then maybe we need to reevaluate our marriage."

He balled his fists and drew a deep breath in. "That's bullshit, Addison… and you know it."

"No. What I know is that I've already been down this road once… with the lying and the deceit, and I really don't plan to go down it again," she said, the words pouring out of her slow and steady.

"Fine," he told her. "I promise I won't see her again."

Addison shook her head. "You shouldn't make promises you can't keep."

"You're one to talk."

"Fuck you."

Minutes went by with neither of them speaking. The silence ate at William. He hated when she gave him the cold shoulder.

"I said I was sorry," he told her. "And I meant it."

"I want to believe you," she relented. She glanced over at him. "But even still—things between us have just been so... off lately."

He shrugged. "So, let's fix that."

She sighed and then looked away. "If only it were that easy."

~

BY THE TIME THEY'D SETTLED BACK STATESIDE, WILLIAM WAS both surprised and not surprised to find his face plastered all over the various news outlets. The media had taken Paul's wife's story and run with it—a story, which portrayed a man, so hackneyed at the hands of his grueling and unrelenting boss that he worked himself to death, *literally.*

With William front and center playing the villain, it turned out to be a sensational news story on the pursuit of success—no matter the cost. At first, he'd done his best to shrug it off—as nothing more than a story that just so happened to hit at the right time. But as the days wore on, and the rift in his marriage deepened, it clearly took its toll on him.

After all, who was he to argue? He *was* at least partially to blame for Paul's death. *The truth was he never should have let him get on that plane.*

Even though the coroner had found no determinative cause of death and deemed the autopsy incomplete, pending toxicology—this fact mattered little to the media. To make matters worse, his wife had barely said a word to him since arriving home, and for the life of him, he couldn't figure out how to move toward reconciliation.

In addition, he'd received another letter that afternoon. This one also left on his windshield. He read and then re-read the note, his palms covered in sweat.

We are both scared.

It matters not

That only one of us

Is willing to admit it.

Finally, the flashback came and he understood why his heart felt as though it just might leap out of his chest.

He must have been around eight at the time. He'd asked and then begged his mother to pick him up from school the way she used to—at the very least, to be there when he arrived home.

"I'm scared," he'd told her over breakfast the one morning of many that she had managed to make it downstairs before he left for school.

She looked at him point blank, and then back at her magazine. He waited, holding his breath, watching as she flipped through several pages before responding. "You're scared?" she asked, and she lowered the magazine to meet his eye. "You know, William, I have responsibilities—other than just hanging around this kitchen. Men like your stepfather expect their women to act, and more importantly, to look a certain way..." she told him with a heavy sigh.

"But—" he started. He wanted to tell her what was happening and he would have had she not cut him off.

She held up one finger. "You'll see when you're older. I expect you'll be that kind of man yourself," she told him. "So don't whine to me about being scared. You aren't the one in danger of being replaced! The world doesn't revolve around you."

"He—"

"Damn it," she said, slamming the magazine on the table. "You just don't get it, do you?" she asked casually, softening her tone. "All of this…" she said, waving her hands in the air. "It's all for you."

And that memory is how William once again found himself at Sondra's doorstep.

~

CHAPTER FOURTEEN

10:32 AM

Dearest William,

I did you a solid on this one and for that, you should be glad. I know it's caused quite a bit of trouble for you, but what you should know is that was never my intention. It was a mere side effect, and maybe, in this case, I was the teacher and you were the lesson. But we'll save that for another day.

That woman was trouble, William. She was a thorn in your side and that made her a thorn in mine. Here's the thing... Right is right. Wrong is wrong. And someone has to protect the innocent. In this case, that someone turned out to be me. That's what you should take away from this my dear. I will always and forever protect you. Together we are a team.

I'll be your Bonnie; you'll be my Clyde.

Paul is dead. But it isn't your fault. It's mine. Which is why I did what any good and faithful person would do and took matters into my own hands to set the record straight. I broke into her house and I waited. I watched her going about her day and I stalked my prey. I liked her house. It felt rather cozy being there.

Mostly, because she was one of those crazy meticulous neat freaks in which everyone and everything had to have its place. She didn't seem like a grieving widow to me. She hummed and she cleaned, and she slept. But she never seemed all that sad. Poor Paul. No wonder he'd so easily turned to me. He was desperate because he was so clearly starved. This woman probably never, in the whole of their marriage, loved him the way I'd done in half an hour.

It was this reason alone that for nearly a full day, I snuck around her house, moving about and rearranging things—all the while letting her think she was going nuts. I made noises and let her search for me. We played hide and seek. It was fun while it lasted. But eventually, I let her find me.

She was one of those crazy bitches, the kind in the movies who go looking for trouble and then wonders why they end up dead.

Even still, she was a fun one, my love.

I wanted her to hurt like she was hurting you. I wanted her to feel it. That's why I drugged her and I waited. I filled her with my poison, and then I reveled in her terror. She didn't know what was happening to her, but she was smart enough to realize she was losing control. They always do… after it's too late.

She put up a good fight, this one, I'll tell you that much. She was stronger than her husband was—and I have to give her props for that.

But she was lazy. That was her mistake. She wanted something for nothing. She wanted to take what wasn't hers to take via the mess that is our current legal system.

I saved you thousands, if not millions in litigation fees, love!

You should be thanking me!

Anyhow, once she was groggy, I moved in. I hid in her closet, knocked boxes of shoes off her pristine rack, and then let her come searching. You should have seen the look on her face when I lunged at her. She fought me, but I came out on top. I always do. When I placed the cord around her neck, you should have seen the look on her face. Her eyes nearly popped out of her head! I told her if she stopped struggling, I'd release the cord and so eventually, she did. She screamed a few times and I tightened. Loosened, then tightened. Lather, rinse, repeat.

By the fourth go 'round, my message finally sunk in.

Then, once she understood our little agreement, I used the rope I'd brought to tie her to one of the chairs in her dining room. She was compliant. They're usually a little more compliant by this point. Next, they want to be friends. They believe it's their ticket out of the mess they've found themselves in.

So, now that we were mostly on the same page, over the next forty-eight hours or so, we had loads of fun. I told her all about you, and how her greed and selfishness was ruining your life. I told her the story of our love and she listened. But that wasn't enough. You see, she doubted that she was going to die and that was a mistake.

She thought she could win, that she could beat me at my own game, and she was wrong. Dead wrong.

If there's one thing a hostage hates more than anything—it's the complete and utter loss of control. Like so many of the others, I terrorized her by taking her freedoms.

I gave her water and then made her urinate on herself when she had to go. After a bit of sitting in her own piss, she got nervous. She started to think I might actually be crazy. Clearly, we weren't friends. After all, what kind of friend makes someone sit in his or her own piss? And this is the point at which they all get nervous, my dear. Reality starts to set in. And here's what happens—they shit themselves. I don't know how or why—but it happens. Every. Single. Time. I think I read once that it's the body's way of preparing itself to die. Anyway, so she shits on herself, she's wet, she's gross, and this is one position no one ever expects to be found in, so she does what any rational person would do and begins the bargaining process.

I told her I only wanted to make her sick. I told her it was best if I got her drunk so that we could forget any of this ever happened. We came up with a plan. She would get so drunk she'd forget, and then she'd sign a paper I'd typed up saying that she was withdrawing the lawsuit. Just these two itty-bitty consolations and she could go free. I promised. But I crossed my fingers behind my back, the way I always do. And she actually agreed!

From there, I made her drink the bottle of whiskey in her liquor cabinet, shot by glorious shot. And when she threw it up, I made her sustain herself on her own vomit for a full day. I know it sounds horrible and it was. Especially for me. I force-fed her and she began to fight again. She said she was sorry and would drop the suit. She said that she just missed her husband— but it wasn't enough. She was a liar. And she needed to join Paul, wherever it is that dead people and liars go.

Eventually, the weekend and thus, our time together was nearing an end (I had to work!). So, I untied her from the chair and then drug her by her hair to the bathroom. I placed her in the tub and filled it with water. She whined so much, William. You wouldn't believe it. *'Please don't do this! Please! I'll do anything, please, if you just let me live.'* Blah, blah, *blah—they never do come up with anything original.*

Her begging was so incessant that I nearly drowned her. But I didn't.

Nope.

She deserved a painful death. She deserved to suffer. Just the way she made you suffer. I held her under the water and dunked her again and again, over and over, and boy, did she ever thrash and kick about. She made such a mess! For that alone, I wanted her to pay! I held her under until she passed out. And it took way longer than I thought. Have you ever seen someone nearly drown, William?

It's more peaceful than it sounds, really. As I wore her down, I stared into those shit colored eyes of hers, and I told her she shouldn't have done this. I told her that she'd caused her own demise, but people like her never learn.

They're takers, my love. They're bottom feeders and that is exactly what she ended up being.

Once she'd quit fighting, I did what I had to do. I let the water out and washed her body. I didn't want to go through the extra shit (pun intended!) of getting her clean, but I didn't mind so much. This was the kind of thing I used to do for my father and so it brought some comfort. I removed her soiled clothing, which I would later toss in the wash. Then I used a washcloth to cleanse her naked body. She looked nice lying there like that. Like a canvas awaiting its artist.

After I'd gotten her clean, I refilled the tub, and then slit her wrist. It was a more suitable cause of death than drowning and the medical examiner would never know because both seemed completely logical when you're drunk and have just lost your husband. I knew suicide would be listed as the primary cause. The little issue of water in the lungs, just a by-product of killing herself in the bath.

I laughed at my ingenuity and I cut deeper. The cutting is always my favorite part. It's really something, you know, watching the blood drain out of a person. Watching the water go from mostly clear to a brilliant bright shade of red brought me such joy. It filled me up and gave me the strength I needed to finish the job. After all, I had quite a bit of cleaning ahead of me, and now such a short window of time in which to get it done.

For your wife had just rang and asked me to meet for dinner. She informed me she had just acquired a new client who needed staffing right away. It mattered little that I was the mastermind (and the real person) behind this fictitious client. You see, this was a test. And she sort of failed. Her problem was that she had learned to rely on me—because I had become the kind of person that she trusted to always, no matter what, get the job done. She'd even said as much on the phone.

And just like that, another of our problems had begun to resolve itself.

Yours truly,

L

P.S. Another poem for you:

I've never wanted anything more,

Than to be your everything.

To have you look at me.

And know deep down

In your bones—

In all the ways that count

that I was enough.

~

CHAPTER FIFTEEN

William glanced down at the table in his conference room and then up at the men sitting opposite him. For cops, they appeared rather blasé. Clearly, it had been awhile since either of them had spent any time on the beat. The smaller of the two studied William's face. He was a small man, who upright, couldn't have been over five and a half feet tall. His red hair and deep brown eyes lent him an angry, hungry expression, and William guessed he'd be the first to speak. The older and larger of the two was hunched over gazing at his phone. He wore an expression on his face of boredom. It was clear he cared little about the reason they were there.

William studied the men and did his best to focus on what was being said, but it took concentrated effort to do so. The harder he tried to focus, the more his vision seemed to blur, and in turn, he gave up and resumed staring at the table. Occasionally he looked up, the last thing he wanted to do was to appear guilty. But mostly, he studied the lines in the oak and willed himself to stay awake. He hadn't slept much at all over the past forty-eight hours, as the flashbacks had been rampant. Things had gotten so bad that he'd thought a visit with Sondra would help—only it hadn't. To make matters worse, she'd fucked up—she'd agreed to see him, but she was angry and distracted and ultimately, she'd swung the belt and missed, leaving him with a black eye.

Knowing his wife would question the injury, he'd texted her to say that he was working late and then made sure to duck out early this morning before she'd awoken. Still, he knew he couldn't hide forever.

As he'd predicted, the smaller of the two detectives was the first to address him directly. "Can you tell us your whereabouts over the weekend?" he asked. "Beginning with last night?"

William eyed his attorney who nodded, a sign that it was okay to answer. "I was working last night..." he said. "Most of the rest of the weekend was spent with my family."

The redhead listened to his response and then began jotting something down on the notepad in front of him.

William cleared his throat. He leaned in and loosened his tie. "Why?" he asked eventually. "What's this about? I've already told you everything I know about Paul..."

The man's seemingly angry eyes met his. He cleared his throat. "With whom might we verify that you were working last night?"

"Hold on," his attorney interjected. "Before my client answers any further questions, I would like to know exactly why you've called this meeting."

"We just need to get a few facts straight."

William watched as his attorney shifted. "As my client mentioned, he's already given you all of the information he has in regards to Mr. Mayfield's sudden death."

"What happened to your eye?" The older and less interested detective chimed in.

William looked over at his attorney. He wasn't going to answer because he couldn't be truthful.

The redhead continued jotting down notes while he peered up at William.

"Again," his attorney said. "My client isn't answering any further questions until you tell us what this is about."

The redheaded detective spoke slowly, carefully. William already knew he didn't like him, but this fact became even more apparent as his beady eyes focused in on William's face expectantly as he spoke. "Paul Mayfield's wife was found dead late last night. We have reason to believe her death may not have been accidental."

William swallowed hard. He hadn't expected that.

The detective continued. "So," he said before pausing and continuing, "that's why it's imperative we confirm your whereabouts over the past forty-eight hours."

William's attorney slunk back in his chair. "I'm not sure what this has to do with my client, other than the fact that her husband had been an employee of his."

"Well, for one, her husband expired while on a business trip with Mr. Hartman. We don't yet have an exact cause of death. And two, we understand Mrs. Mayfield had recently filed a lawsuit against your client over the matter."

William gazed over the detective's shoulder, beyond him, and out the high-rise window.

His attorney leaned in, clasped his hands together and rested them on the table. "Gentlemen, my client has given you the information he has. As he has informed you, he was working last night and was with his family all weekend long. I have no doubt you'll be able to verify this information in due time. For now, he's a busy man, as are we all—so if it's all the same to you—I'd say it's about time that we conclude this visit."

The men murmured something that appeared to be agreement and then stood. His attorney followed suit.

William remained seated and glassy-eyed as he stared out the window.

He hadn't a clue what happened to Paul's wife.

But what he did know was this was the last thing he needed.

~

WILLIAM STARED AT THE FLOOR.

"William?"

He looked up at the man sitting opposite him. Wearing an expression of defiance, he stood his ground. "Like I told you —I can't say."

His attorney let him finish as he leaned back in his chair and then forward again, placing his palms on the table. He spread his fingers apart, then brought them together again as he seemed to consider the best way to respond. "William, you do realize how bad it's going to look if you continue to refuse to give the *who, where,* and *what* of your whereabouts last night. I hate to have to say it, but I'm afraid this tactic is going to invite more trouble than you're looking for. 'Trust me' isn't exactly an answer these guys buy into…"

William shook his head. "I know my rights, counselor. I don't have to tell them anything I don't want to. Besides, they don't have anything on me. There's no way they could."

"In this case, unfortunately, I'm going to advise you— as your attorney—and also as a friend, that your cooperation is essential. The cops can either make this investigation go away quickly or they can and *will* make your life hell until you give them what they want."

He shrugged. "I just don't feel the need to say where I was."

His attorney let out an exaggerated sigh. He started to speak and then hesitated. He removed his glasses, placed them on the table, and pinched the bridge of his nose between two fingers. "Then I'm going to have to ask you point blank if you have something to hide."

William stood and walked to the floor to ceiling window, which overlooked the city below. He crossed his arms and pondered the best way to respond while he watched the hustle and bustle going on many stories down at street level. He took a deep breath in and let it out before answering. "I guess, technically, the answer to that would be yes—but it's not what you think. I had nothing to do with that woman's death."

Finally, he turned to face his attorney and looked him straight in the eye.

The man seemed genuinely relieved. "I see." He pursed his lips. "Or I think I do, anyway... let me put it another way then. Let me ask you this. Would this technicality be something you're hiding from your wife?"

He frowned. "Something like that."

The attorney nodded in understanding. "In that case, I hate to say it—but you need to talk to her. And you need to tell her the truth. Because I'm afraid that one way or another, it will inevitably come out. It always does."

William nodded. "That's exactly what I was afraid of."

◊

CHAPTER SIXTEEN

Twenty-four hours missing

William rubbed his eyes. He'd been staring at his computer screen for God knows how long. Everything blurred together and trying to concentrate proved futile. He slunk back in this chair, closed his eyes, and at some point, realized he must have fallen asleep.

He awoke to find Sondra standing on the opposite side of his desk with her hands on her hips. "What. The. Fuck?" she demanded.

Pondering his next move, he sat upright and yawned. Noting her icy glare, he said nothing until she finally spoke again.

"Why in the fuck did you insist on putting me in the middle of your marital issues? I told you to talk to her and you had so many chances, William…"

"I don't know what you want me to say."

Sondra shook her head. "Do you realize what kind of position you put me in here? You had to know that she'd come to me and how she'd react when she did…"

He sighed. "I know and—".

Sondra shifted her stance. "I'm her boss. What did you expect would happen?"

He had nothing. "What did *you* expect would happen?"

"I expected that you'd fucking man up and tell your wife that you were having issues."

"Yeah, well, I didn't expect that when she confronted you... you'd tell her to take a few days off to get away," he responded his voice sounding every bit as bitter as he'd meant it to be. "How did you suppose that would help the situation any?"

She exhaled and looked away. "She's not taking my calls."

"Mine either," he scoffed.

She looked at him directly then. "Where did she say she was going?"

"She didn't tell me exactly," he said, shaking his head. "But her friend, Jess, said she'd called to ask her if she could use her family's beach house. You know... I wanted to give her a little bit of space to cool off, but if she doesn't answer my calls within the next hour or so... I'm heading down there."

"Maybe you just need to give her some time," Sondra advised. She sighed heavily. "It's a lot to digest and she was pretty angry."

William met her gaze directly. "You're telling me."

~

THE DETECTIVE ADJUSTED HIS GLASSES BEFORE SPEAKING. "WAS your wife upset the last time you saw her?"

William eyed his attorney with irreverence. He glanced around his office as he considered the question and how much he wanted to say. Finally, he met the detective's glare. "Yes," he answered, careful to keep his tone neutral.

He found his tone mattered little in the end. His answer

was met with an all too familiar nod of recognition. William knew this expression very well. He understood the officer had already made up his mind about what had happened and why—before having ever asked the first question. He'd connected the dots, just the way he wanted them connected. Satisfied, the officer jotted down a note and adjusted his pen, more for the sake of doing so than because it needed to be adjusted.

He waited for William to elaborate, and when he didn't offer any more, the officer pressed on. "And what was she upset about?"

He shrugged. "Standard stuff."

"Which would be?"

William drew in a long breath and held it. He hated answering these questions. *It was no one's goddamned business —what had happened was between him and his wife.* Some things were simply private. Biding his time, he exhaled slowly. "I'd rather not say."

"Then why exactly *did* you request this meeting?"

William swallowed hard in an attempt to push down the emotion that threatened to bubble up to the surface. *He had to maintain control.* He knew he had to stay calm. He pursed his lips and steadied his breathing before replying. "Because I wanted to make sure I get my point across... I don't think you guys are taking me seriously," he admitted. "And because I don't trust you. As you know... I have my own team working to find my wife. But I like to hit things from all sides... and I don't want to miss anything here."

"This has happened before?" The officer asked although he knew the answer.

William's jaw set. "That's exactly why the sooner we find her, the better. Addison wouldn't just disappear on her family like this. Especially not on her children. Which means the clock is ticking, and quite frankly, everyone in this room knows that with each passing hour, the situation looks more and more grim."

"This all sounds like a bit of déjà vu to me," a second officer said.

William didn't respond.

"And *where* do *you* think your wife could be, Mr. Hartman? Other than the beach house, that is," a detective asked. He glanced down at his watch. "I can't say you've really given us much to go on."

"I've told you what I know."

"Maybe," he replied. "But we still have many unanswered questions about where you were the evening of Donna Mayfield's murder."

William clenched his jaw as he ran his finger along the length of the edge of his desk. *He wanted it to hurt, but it didn't. Just one sharp corner was all he needed. Something just to feel anything other than what he felt. He needed the real thing. Something to ease the rage that had built up inside him which was threatening to unleash itself at any moment.* "I was with my business partner that night."

"Your business partner?"

"Yes."

The officer cocked his head. "Why didn't you tell us this before?"

"Because my business partner happens to be a woman. One which my wife doesn't particularly like."

The scrawny detective smiled like he hit the jackpot. William knew how it looked. Missing wife. Secret meetings with another woman…"And this woman's name is…?" He looked down at his notepad and back at William. "You know, we'll need to verify…"

William produced Sondra's business card from his back pocket and handed it to the detective. *He'd known to come prepared.*

The redheaded man nodded slowly. It was a weak attempt at feigning understanding. He pushed up from the chair he'd been perched on, checked his watch, and patted his partner on the back as an order for him to follow. "Well, that certainly makes a little bit more sense," he exclaimed.

He waited for William to respond and when he didn't, he took it upon himself to ensure they were on the same page. "See..." he remarked. "*Now*, I think you're getting the hang of the way this works—you help us, we help you. In fact—" he started and then paused to grin as though a brilliant idea had just come upon him. "I tell you what... we'll give you some time to think it over, see if there is anything you can remember about the little spat you had... I mean, it's hardly *even* been a full day... and, well, you know how women can be when it comes to other women..." He trailed off just long enough to let a patronizing chuckle escape. "She's probably just somewhere cooling off. Who knows? She could turn up back home before the sun goes down. Tell you what—how about I give you a ring in the morning once I get this all checked out with..." He squinted as he glanced at the card and then looked back up at William. "With um... Sondra... and we can discuss next steps then—that is, if she hasn't turned up."

William didn't take his eyes off the man as he picked up the tumbler in front of him, which had been chilled exactly to his liking. He gulped the water down trying to erase the familiar metallic taste of blood, which had filled his mouth. He'd bitten his tongue hard—primarily to stop himself from pummeling the bastard and his blasé attitude, but also to hold in all the things he'd almost said. The least of them being—that his wife wasn't going to turn up by sundown.

She wasn't going to just turn up... because something bad had happened—that much he was sure of.

And, unfortunately for William, he was also smart enough

to know what deep, deep shit he was in if he didn't come up with some answers soon.

~

LYDIA STRAIGHTENED HER SKIRT AND THEN DOUBLE-CHECKED her appearance in the elevator mirror. She hated skirts. But she knew *he* loved them—so she'd made an effort. That morning, she dressed up—even more so than normal. She put on her brand new heels and she played the part.

It was the least she could do, really.

Once she reapplied Addison's lipstick, she kissed the mirror for good measure. She exited the elevator, and waltzed into that office like a woman on a mission.

And she was.

This was the beginning of a new era for her and so she wore gold to signify the glory that had now become hers for the taking.

Only no one noticed her in all her glory. Not even *him.*

They were all too busy, all so stupid looking for and talking about *her,* rushing about like they were. Everything that day turned out to be all about Addison. It was 'Addison this' and 'Addison that.'

But no one had even thought to ask her any questions in all of the fuss.

Which was a damned shame, really.

Not only because these days she'd come to know Addison Hartman better than anyone—but also because she held all the answers.

~

CHAPTER SEVENTEEN

Seventeen Days Missing

10:15 AM

Dearest William,

It's getting late. It's getting so very late.

The clock is ticking and time is running out.

I didn't want it to have to get to this point.

I didn't want to tell you these things.

I thought I would be out of this place by now.

I didn't want to have to force your hand.

But I do.

It's time to make a choice.

You see, I didn't want to take her.

I really didn't.

You have to know that!

Just as I told the detectives, we met and she told me she needed to get away. She said things were going south between the two of you and that she needed to get away for a few days to clear her head. And I know she told you as much, too. She was scared of you, love. I can't be sure, and perhaps she never said it directly—but it was definitely implied. And facts are facts, and the fact is she knew too much. So I helped her 'disappear.' It's a long story, but as you know, she's still missing.

And while we're on the subject of facts, let me inform you of another—the police aren't going to help you because they don't like you. More importantly, they don't believe you. They may think I'm just another random nut job. But they think *you're* a killer. And no matter how many times they question me—in their minds, if your wife didn't in fact flee because she was afraid of you—and something bad *did* happen, well, the fact is you're still suspect numero uno.

That's a problem for both you and your wife. That's why they aren't looking for her, not *really* anyway.

I want to tell you everything, but it's important that you hear my side, too. And here's the truth, if you aren't willing to listen, then there is the very real possibility that your wife will die. As you likely know, I was scheduled to have a hearing today in court to decide whether or not they can legally keep me in here. But that got delayed. The court system is the biggest mess I've ever seen. They need the likes of me to work out their kinks! Suffice it to say, I'm not a happy camper, William. At this point, you've had me locked away in here for fourteen days. Your wife had enough to eat for maybe nine of those—eleven if she was smart enough to consider rationing.

You do the math.

That said, I think maybe it's time you paid me a visit.

Do you realize that she and I had spent the better part of three glorious days together before you had me put in here? One of which you knew about—but two of them you don't. I know things you would appreciate knowing, too. In fact, there are letters she wrote to you during our little soirée. And I think that you should have them. If you visit, I will tell you where they are—and if you're really as intelligent as I believe you to be—then you'll listen and you'll understand where I'm coming from. You need to understand my position. Not just now. But all along. And maybe... just maybe... I'll tell you where your wife is.

Before it's too late.

I know how you feel about me. And it's time, William. It is time for the sake of everyone involved that you own up to those feelings so we can bring them out into the light.

Is it risky for me to be putting this all down on paper? Sure. Will you take this to the cops? Of course you will.

But here's what you should know, William. One, I'll never tell. Not until you understand. Two, like the court system, the cops fuck everything up. They'll slow the process, they have their ways, and your wife will starve to death. And three, I'm being held because they believe me to be insane. Because you had me put here! I believe the appropriate diagnosis, or at least the one they've handed down, is Borderline Personality Disorder. Who knows, though. Every time I talk to someone new, they tell me something different. Different day, different diagnosis.

Basically, in laymen's terms, I'm a psychopath.

And, my love, everyone knows psychopaths often have trouble discerning fact from fiction.

No worries though, when I see you we'll get it all sorted out.

I will be in touch.

Yours truly,

L

~

CHAPTER EIGHTEEN

Seventy-Two Hours Missing

As William rushed through the automatic doors, the cold, sterile aroma hit him like anesthetic straight to his heart. The scent overwhelmed his senses taking him back to the dozens of times he showed up in this very place as a kid with injuries no one seemed to question. *He was just an active boy, they'd said.*

Still, he searched the ER frantically having received the text from Sondra that he needed to head there.

He made his way to the window marked 'Check In' and knocked hastily on the glass. "Addison Hartman. I'm looking for my wife. Her name is Addison Hartman," he said urgently.

The nurse tilted her head to the side and then hesitantly checked her screen before meeting his gaze. "I'm afraid I don't have anyone here by that name," she told him.

"How about Sondra Sheehan? Can you check for that one?"

She gave him the once over before glancing back at her

screen. "Just a moment," she said, sliding the glass window shut. He watched as she picked up the phone, although he couldn't hear what was being said. The room began to spin, and he compensated by bending over and placing his palms on his knees. He'd run through the parking lot to the emergency room lobby, he'd already been slightly winded. Nervous. Now he was doubled over, out of breath, and very near a panic attack.

Finally, the double-doors buzzed and the nurse opened the glass window once more. "Through those doors and to the right," she said. "That'll take you to the nurses' station. They'll direct you from there."

He made his way wild-eyed to the nurses' station. There, an oversized man ushered him to follow. They rounded a corner, and then another, until eventually the corridors all looked the same. The man stopped so suddenly at the entrance to one of the rooms, that William nearly ran into the back of him. The man moved forward so hesitantly, William worried maybe he was afraid something might jump out at them. He peered around the curtain, and when he apparently deemed it safe, he stepped aside to make way for William to enter. As he stepped into the dimly lit room, he saw Sondra lying on the bed, eyes closed, her arm in a sling.

He glanced around the room and spoke in a near whisper. "What in the hell is going on?"

She opened her eyes slowly as though she'd expected to see him standing there. "I found your stalker," she said. "That's what's going on." She raised her arm and then lowered it slowly, her face twisted in pain. "And I guess you could say," Sondra winced, "that she didn't take kindly to being found."

"What?" William narrowed his gaze. "Where is Addison?"

"That I don't know."

William moved further into the small room. He stopped at her bedside, and searched her face.

"But I know who probably does," she told him. She inhaled slowly and then shifted, wincing in pain as she moved. "Lydia," she murmured. "Addison's assistant. She's the one who's been sending you the letters."

"So Addison isn't here?" he asked, shaking his head. "They haven't found her?"

"No."

William turned away. He ran his fingers through his hair and then paced the length of the small room.

Sondra cleared her throat. "Where do I even start?"

"At the beginning."

She raised her brow. "Ok," she said. "But first you need to calm down."

"I am calm," he replied stopping in his tracks.

"I went to talk with Lydia, seeing that she is both an employee of mine *and* the last person to see Addison. I figured it would be a good place to start."

"Lydia?" he asked, cutting her off.

"I wanted to discuss a few things with her."

"Lydia," he said again.

"Are you going to let me finish or not?"

She waited and when she was satisfied she had his attention she continued. "I'd never really spent any time with her to be honest. Anyway... once the questions started, she started acting really funny. Standoffish, combative, and then... she just sort of lost it. She lunged at me and placed her hands around my throat, very nearly choking me to death. All the while, she was repeating over and over how this was all my fault. She said I was the one stealing you away from her and Addison. I had no clue what she was talking about—which leads me to my next question..."

William cocked his head.

"Have you been having an affair with this woman?"

His eyes widened. "No," he scoffed. "I hardly know her."

"Hmmm," Sondra uttered, pressing her lips to one another. "Because as of about an hour ago, our IT department found some pretty questionable material on her hard drive in regards to you. Photos," she said. "Thousands of them... letters, drafts of letters, it was... well, a lot. And very disturbing," she added. "To say the least."

He pursed his lips. "So she must know where Addison is."

"I assume, yes."

"So where is she? Lydia?"

"Here. Somewhere. Or at least I think, anyway. I managed to get out from underneath her and break the grip she had around my neck," she told him.

William resumed pacing. He did his best thinking that way. "Good thing you're trained for that."

Sondra shrugged. "She still managed to break my arm, but I messed her up pretty badly—"

He deadpanned. "How badly?"

"I would have killed her if building security hadn't gotten there when they did. And here's the thing, William. I've seen a lot of monsters in my time, but I've never seen anyone with eyes as dark as hers. She just... snapped. That woman is a psychopath."

"Great," he said. "We've established that. But can she talk? I mean... we need to find out what she's done with Addison."

"I'm hurt," Sondra told him feigning shock. "It's like you don't even care what she did to me."

"I care very much," he corrected. He knew this was her way of being a smart ass and he wasn't in the mood for games. "It's an indication of what she might do to my wife. So—I need to know—can she talk?"

"She could except, get this—she's claiming to have been having an affair with you."

"Sondra—" William said, cutting her off. "I don't care what she claims. I'm only interested in facts."

Sondra opened her mouth to speak and then closed it. "Well—" she started. "In that case, she claims that your wife found out and took off. She says Addison is afraid of you and that she attacked me in self-defense because... you and I are also having an affair. She claims that I was going to fire her, that I was the first to strike, by backhanding her, which is why she acted in the manner she did."

William shook his head and let out a long sigh. "Still, not exactly facts," he commented, staring at the IV bag hanging beside her bed. "Do they have you on narcotics."

Sondra didn't answer his question. She knew he wanted her to cut to the chase. So she did. "She's filed temporary restraining orders on the three of us. She says she fears for her life. And basically, it's our word against hers."

He inhaled deeply and then let it out. "What the fuck..."

She swallowed. "Yeah."

"What about the letters she left on my car... and all that stuff you guys found on her computer?" he demanded, pacing faster now.

Sondra shook her head. "I don't know... the cops say they're looking into it."

"Yeah, well, let me speak to her."

She bit her lip. "I'm afraid that's going to be a problem. There's a restraining order in place—which means you can't."

～

WILLIAM, ONCE AGAIN, FOUND HIMSELF SITTING ADJACENT TO the two detectives. This time at the local police station.

He placed his head in his hands and waited for his attorney to arrive. *Don't say anything, he reminded himself.*

The officers made small talk, offering him coffee and

other beverages, but he declined and attempted to focus once more on putting the pieces together. He combed through the argument he had with Addison, and there was nothing he could pinpoint that would explain the fact that she still hadn't turned up. He went over and over that final conversation. *Had she been angry?* Sure. *Enough to leave him for good?* Maybe. *But to leave her children this long without calling?* Never.

At last, the door opened and William breathed a sigh of relief. He didn't like not knowing where his wife was. He didn't like having to look his stepchildren in the face and lie to them, telling them their mother was away on business. Any day now, he was going to have to tell them the truth. But most of all, he hated the feeling that everyone thought he was guilty. In his mind, they'd already condemned him as yet another man who'd cheated on his wife and then buried her body. The very idea that anyone believed he could hurt Addison made him sick. Thinking that someone else had—or might be now—well, it was too much for him to take. Sitting in that horribly lit, grungy, cold room at the police station didn't help matters any. It was all he could do not to lose it. He wanted out, he wanted to do something, to find her, and there was nothing he could do but sit in that room practically crawling out of his skin. *Waiting.* It had been a long time since William had felt this helpless, not since he was a kid at the hands of his stepfather. Here his wealth didn't matter. He was just another husband whose wife had gone missing. He either wasn't giving— or couldn't give —them the answers they wanted which meant that to them he was a suspect. Here, he was guilty due to the mere fact of statistics. *It's always the husband.*

The redheaded, beady-eyed detective cleared his throat, looked to William's attorney, and then back at him. "So I guess we can finally begin…"

The attorney's bottom lip jutted out as he gave a slight nod.

"Can you tell us again about the last time you saw your wife? Giving as much detail as possible…"

William swallowed and then took a deep breath. "It's just as I said. I came home from the office. It was late. We had—"

"What time?" The second detective asked.

"Around 10 PM."

"Go on…" The redhead urged.

"We made love. Everything was fine."

"I thought the two of you fought."

"We argued," William corrected. *Choice of words were important, he knew.*

"Okay. So, the two of you argued. Why?"

William sighed. "She turned on the light and saw that I'd been injured. She was upset that I hadn't been honest about the injury."

"And then?"

"And then she told me that she was leaving the following morning." He paused trying to remember her precise wording. "She said she thought it was best that she go to the beach for a few days. A friend of hers has a house there…"

"Why did you lie about the injury?"

"She didn't like the fact that I was involved in violent activities."

"You mean with the other woman… the, um… Dominatrix."

"My business partner. Yes, as she's told you, she's a Dominatrix."

"Your wife used to be a Dominatrix herself, did she not?"

"Yes."

"Yes, she was?"

"That's correct."

"Then why would she have a problem with it?"

"I don't know. We didn't get that far."

"Because you lied?"

William closed his eyes and reopened them slowly. "Like I said, I don't know."

"You don't know or you don't want to say?"

He tensed. "I don't know."

The detective checked his notes. "Your wife's assistant last saw her alive and well on the twenty-fifth. Can you tell us your whereabouts that day?"

"I was at the office."

"From what time to what time?"

William shifted. "I don't remember."

"You don't remember?"

"I'd have to check my schedule. I can't tell you off the top of my head. It's all logged."

"I see. Well, is there *anything* you *can* tell us about that day…"

"I don't know. I mean… she wasn't taking my calls. I was desperate to speak to her. I thought she was overreacting… and I just wanted to resolve the situation."

"Overreacting about you seeing another woman, you mean?"

"I wasn't *seeing* another woman."

"Can you tell us about your relationship with Mrs. Sheehan?"

"I'd rather not."

"And with Lydia Hammons?"

"Lydia Hammons?" He cocked his head to the side and narrowed his gaze.

"Yes."

"Don't you mean Lydia Hagel?"

The detective shuffled and then checked the paperwork in front of him. "No," he replied pointing. "I show her legal name here as being Hammons."

William drew a deep breath. His stomach turned. "Oh, my God."

The detective eyed him suspiciously. "Is there a problem?"

His hand flew to his mouth momentarily before he thought to remove it. His mind raced and it was another full minute before he was able to speak. "Are you aware of the case with Scott Hammons? The man who attempted to murder my wife and I?"

The redhead picked up the stack of papers and shuffled them. He searched through a few pausing to read here and there. "Um... no... maybe... okay... *vaguely*."

"Well, if your paperwork there is correct... the two of them share a last name."

~

CHAPTER NINETEEN

Hour Twenty-Four

Dear William,

It's been roughly twenty-four hours now since I was taken from Jessica's beach house to my current undisclosed location. I've been drugged, and I am chained by my ankle to a stake in the center of the room. I was given a notebook and a pen in order to communicate with my captor by slipping notes underneath the door.

This letter has been hidden beneath the plywood floor, which if you're reading it, you obviously know.

I don't know where I am other than that it is dark and damp and smells like a wooded area. For obvious reasons, I will be careful of what I write in the event that these letters are found, but I also will not, in any way, censor myself when it comes to writing about my feelings for you or my family.

I am being kept in a room that is mostly bare. There is a mattress on the floor and a clock on the wall, but that's about it. And I haven't the faintest idea if the time it reads is correct. There's little light, but some does manage to get through tiny cracks in the boarded up window. As I look at that light, and the cracks that let it in, I think of you. I think of the boys. You are my light pouring in. It's funny, except that it isn't. They say that lightning doesn't strike twice and yet here I am being held against my will once again.

It is important that you know what happened to me— and that no matter what happens from here, I want to get a few things straight—

I love you.

I've always loved you. In many ways, I believe I knew it from the very first day we met. And I want you to know I always will.

I also want you to know that I am not being physically abused as of the time of this writing. I have food and I have water. I won't elaborate more than that in case this letter is found before it gets to you, but what I will say is, I am not going down without a fight. I will not be made to say things that I do not mean. I will not negotiate with my captor. Other than trading 'insider info' about your likes and dislikes for the slight possibility that this letter might actually find its way to you, I will not give in to her demands. I will give her nothing more, but I want you to know, that no matter what happens from here on out, I am not afraid. Despite how things have been over the past few months, I have been honored to be your wife.

And if it turns out that I do not make it out of here alive, I want to make sure you don't blame yourself. I know you and I know that will be the case. But it isn't the truth. I also want to ask that you stop running, William. I want you to love again, and the next time, whether it turns out it's with me or it isn't, I want to ask that you give yourself over to it. I own up to the fact that I've made mistakes over the course of the time we've been married. I got so wrapped up in everything and everyone else that I forgot about meeting your needs. I'm sorry for that.

Please, if you get this, know that I love you. Know I am in good spirits, and I am hopeful that I will get out of here alive.

Tell the boys I love them.

Love,

Addison

~

Hour Seventy-Two

BEYOND BEDROCK

Dear William,

It's been three days now. I am counting the hours. Sometimes the minutes. They pass slowly, so slowly. To help pass the time, I have slept a lot. I have not heard from Lydia since early this morning. I heard her car drive away, but she has not returned as of yet. I have plenty of food and water in here. Mostly dry cereal and bottled water. There is a portable potty sort of bucket thing in the corner of the room, but so far, she has not been in to change it. The room is mostly made of wood and it's unfinished. I'm thinking this place is some sort of abandoned cabin, used for hunting, maybe.

Yesterday, Lydia actually spoke with me through the door and there is so much, so many things, William, that I do not understand how I could have missed. I should have seen it. A thousand times, I should have seen it. She's crazy. Perhaps, I was so distracted by the pregnancy and the miscarriage, and then getting back on track afterward that I blatantly missed all of the signs. Were there signs? I don't know.

This is what I know: Lydia believes you are in love with her. From what little she has said to me, she appears to be completely delusional, and I honestly can't say I ever expected this. It is as though I am seeing and hearing a completely different person altogether. This is certainly not the person I hired. She says that she will let me go in time and that she just needs to get over the hump where you realize that I am out of the picture. She says that you need to grieve my loss and that she will help you, and once that is done, and your feelings for all parties have been resolved, that I will be free to go. She believes I am a distraction to your love and to her.

I am tired today, William. I do not believe Lydia, that she will let me go free. The facts don't add up. But I know for my survival that a part of me has to hope. Otherwise, what is the point? As I write, I sit by the window, and although it is boarded up, I manage to get the tiniest bit of light I can. Also, the sounds are somewhat comforting. I have looked for every way possible to get out of here, and so far, I have not found one that does not lie behind the door, which is doubly padlocked from the outside. That much I remember seeing on the way in. I am trying to remember other things, too. But my memory prior to landing in this room is hazy. Nothing seems real, and I feel as though if I don't get out of this room soon, I will lose my mind.

The reality and the loneliness are starting to make me feel very, very empty. Hopefully, Lydia will be back soon and the two of us can talk. I miss you. And I miss the boys. God, I hope you are looking for me.

Love,

Addison

~

Day Four

Dear William,

Lydia still has not returned. I can only hope this is because the police have found out what she has done and that she is in police custody. I pray she is being questioned. Every day I envision her telling you the truth and leading you to me.

I am okay here. Mostly, I sleep when I can. I write you, and it is what keeps me going. It is raining today, it is hot and humid, and I feel as though I might crawl out of my skin. I pace the length of the room and stretch the chain as far as it will go. My leg has begun to bleed where the cuff is attached. I have tried in vain to get free. I try to walk at least five laps around this small space for every hour that I am awake to keep my strength up. I've also started doing push-ups and sit-ups to pass the time. I know I need to stay in fighting shape.

As of late yesterday, I've begun rationing the food and water, which has led to less excrement, a positive due to my waste not being removed from this room. The stench is revolting, although I feel myself growing more and more used to it by the hour. This is what scares me. I do not want to become comfortable here.

To keep me sane, I tell myself stories of you and the boys. It's comforting to recall so many of the good times we had. I also find myself speaking to you aloud. It sounds crazy, but it's nice to hear something, even if it's the sound of my own voice.

I wonder what you guys are doing now, and I hope that you are not too worried. That is what hurts the most. The idea that you and the boys are suffering. Now, I think of all the silly things we argued over and the events that led me to flee to the beach house in the first place, and I am ashamed I let something so irrelevant (in the grand scheme of things) come between us. Not to sweep everything under the rug because there were definite issues, but I guess it just all seems... so ridiculous now that I've come face to face with the very real possibility of never being able to resolve any of it.

Love,
Addison

~

Day Fifteen

Dear William,

Lydia still has not returned. I don't know what is going on, but it appears as though I am being left here to die.

I am almost out of food. There is less than a quarter of a bottle of water left, and I am worried. If that weren't enough to drive a person mad, I am living in my own filth.

Still.

As I wrote yesterday, though, I am not giving up. My appetite has not returned, and as of this morning, I understand why...

I'm pregnant, William.

To say I am shocked would be an understatement.

But I counted the days I've been here against the last time we saw each other and it makes sense that morning sickness would start right about now. Getting my period wasn't something even on my mind until the last few days, when I'd tried to remember when my last one was. Given I don't have my calendar here, I'm not exactly sure, but I'm sure enough to know what this heaviness feels like. There are only a few things in life that can make you feel this tired and most of them have to do with motherhood. It's something you don't forget, this feeling.

Speaking of that, I've been thinking a lot about our last night together. In truth, I think about it every hour of the day. I recall the way you made love to me as though you might swallow me whole, and I miss you so much, William. I remember that we argued about your eye and then I stormed out, and I remember not wanting to go back into the bedroom to get my pills.

Then, when I left the next morning, they were the furthest thing from my mind. Once I'd gotten to the beach, I called the local pharmacy for a refill, but I never made it to pick them up and wound up here instead.

So I guess it all makes sense.

But that doesn't mean I believe it.

In any case, at least now I have something to live for. Something to keep me going.

I just hope someone finds me soon.

Even if that person turns out to be Lydia.

Love,

Addison

~

CHAPTER TWENTY

Eighteen Days Missing (Her)
One Day Free (Me)

Dearest William,

So as you probably know by now... I did it!

I am free, and I am making my way back to your wife. It's taking me a bit longer than I'd hoped (being on the lam has its challenges), but I hope to reach her tomorrow.

It feels so good to be free again. It's actually pretty surprising considering the effort it took me to break away.

You want to know what I had to lose in order to save your wife?

Well, let me tell you.

I almost lost my fucking finger, William!

All for her!

I had it so perfectly planned out, and I executed the plan brilliantly. That's what I want you to know.

You should be so proud!

But, perhaps I'm getting ahead of myself. I began the day by wearing my red sweater to signify strength, passion, and determination. As I awaited my hearing, I thought of you, of our future together, and of all the happy times that we would have to look forward to. I thought about my pinky as I slid my thumb and forefinger over it and it was almost like saying goodbye of sorts. I was saying goodbye to my old life—the one that didn't include you in it every day as the future would. I was sad for just a second there because I considered that you might think a girl with a missing finger would be odd, somehow tarnished, not quite perfect. But then I remembered all the loving ways you'd gazed at me in the time we've known each other, and I realized that's not who you are at all. You're a man who understands brokenness and imperfection—because that's who you are. You're broken and imperfect yourself, and this is something Addison never understood, and this is why I will be with you and she won't.

And then, as I sat in that courtroom, I imagined you rubbing and then kissing the nub where my little finger once met my hand. I got the best tingly sensation all over and it was then I knew it was time. So I wrapped the unwoven thread around my little finger (just like the one you have me wrapped around) and I pulled tight. Just as tight as the pull you have on my heart. So tight, it hurts. It was you I thought about as I watched my finger turn from red to blue to purple, and all the while, I pulled tighter and tighter until I didn't feel a thing. The pain became a part of me, something I could live with, just the way my love for you has. After it was clear (just as it is with the love I feel for you) that there was no turning back and that my finger couldn't be saved, I began to scream. I screamed and I screamed and I screamed.

The next thing I knew, I was being tied and held down in the back of an ambulance en route to the hospital, and I realized that it was only a matter of time. And here's why. The security in hospitals is shit. This isn't my first go-round with it, but I'll elaborate more on that later—when we are together.

At the hospital, they said I would need surgery as the circulation had been cut off for too long, and my finger, unlike our love, was dead and there was nothing they could do other than remove it. But then, they got me in the operating room and I swear, it was a bloody miracle. They were able to somehow save the finger.

What you should know, my love, is that I would have been more than happy to sacrifice that finger in order to gain my freedom.

Because that's just the kind of thing you do for love.

Sometimes—one thing or another simply has to be sacrificed—because there is no other way.

Now, I am on my way back to Addison.

And I hope she hasn't been sacrificed just because you wanted me locked away.

At least then, though, it will be easy. Cut and dry—just the way you like it.

Honestly, you will have no one to blame but yourself.

It will be better for the both of us that way.

Yours eternally,

L

~

Nineteen Days Missing (Her)
Two Days Free (Me)

Dearest William,

You might be pleased to know that ADDISON IS ALIVE.

I couldn't believe it, my love.

A part of me is in complete and utter shock that she could have survived the heat and the lack of food and water, not to mention the filth—but somehow or another, she did.

She has lost a lot of weight though. And she looks sickly.

I know she was happy to see me (or maybe relieved is a better word) even if she wouldn't admit it.

I should probably tell you how she repaid me, though, for all of my hard work trying to get back here to her. It almost makes me wish I'd let her rot, quite honestly. When I opened the padlocks, I found her curled up into a ball in the corner of the room, and for the briefest of moments, I thought she might actually be dead. So I tiptoed in and she doesn't move. She doesn't respond when I call her name… nothing. I go to her and I shake her… and still nothing. Then I turn away and she lunges at me. She grabs me from behind and puts me in a chokehold, and because I am agile and smart and one thousand times stronger than her, I stab her in the forearm with the treat I siphoned off my pharmacy tech friend—just a little something I'd picked up and brought along in case I needed to finish her off. So I push the syringe down and she lets go, her eyes wild and as big as saucers. She stumbles backward, then pulls the needle out, and sinks to the floor. She starts to cry. But she grows more and more limp by the minute, and so she curls back into her little ball, which is a self-protection mechanism, this much I know.

She stays that way and cries for a long while as I stand over her wondering whether or not to finish her off. I pick up the syringe, check what's left, and then I spit on her.

She does not look at me.

She knows I have won.

Still, I tell her as much anyway.

Then I walk away. With as much sedative as I've just sent coursing through her veins, I know she won't follow—she can't follow. I return with just the tiniest bit of water and place it beside her.

And I tell her I won't come back until she has learned to be grateful for everything I've done for her.

Let's just hope (for her sake) that she's still alive by then.

All my love,

L

P.S. I wrote you a little something:

I long for you so much it hurts.
The void you left behind seeps into every part of me.
The depth of it fills my lungs
Until it's difficult to breathe.
And I'm drowning.
In you.

∾

Twenty Days Missing (Her)

Three Days Free (Me)

Dearest William,

I had the most beautiful dream last night.

You and I were on a beach and we were getting married. In my dream, it looked precisely like the wedding photo that sat atop Addison's desk, only I was Addison, and well, it was more amazing than anything I'd ever imagined. When I woke, I realized it was a sign. I knew exactly what it was you were urging me to do. You wanted me to look like Addison. So you will be happy to know that 'Operation Become Addison' has officially commenced. I have done so much research already this morning, and I have the funds and tomorrow I will begin making the necessary appointments to officially start the transformation process. I have found an excellent doctor down in Mexico. And this is wonderful news, my love.

I was so thrilled now that I finally understand what it is that you have been asking of me, that I decided to be nice. I have decided to forgive Addison for her little snafu upon my return.

Also, I need something from her in order to fulfill your request.

I need to study her. I need photos. Nude photos. I need to learn her mannerisms. I have a plan!

Lastly, and, this should make you happy, too—my finger is finally feeling a little better. I will mail these letters soon.

But first, I have to get down to Mexico.

Love you mucho grande,

L

~

Dear William,

Sadly, my happiness has waned from this afternoon.

And it is all your wife's fault.

She is testing me.

I know she is scared, and I know she wants food, but what I don't understand is why she insists on fighting me every step of the way. If I weren't so angry, I might actually be impressed. So there's that. I did at least learn one thing from her today. And that is just how stubborn she can be.

It is hot here. The stench in her room is overwhelming. She has been sick (hostages and their nerves, I swear) and it is disgusting. So, I did what any smart captor would do, and I entered her room with a water hose. I assumed she would still be groggy, but there she was, sitting up alert—like she'd been expecting me. Which made me angry. She didn't apologize. She didn't say she was glad to see me. She just stared. I tossed a few sponges and cleaning supplies in her direction. Then I pointed to the mess, and I told her to have at it. Only she didn't budge. She just sat there as though maybe I were speaking a language she didn't understand. I took the high-pressure hose and I sprayed her. The filth was coming off one way or another! I expected after a few seconds she'd comply, but she didn't. You see, this is the problem with spoiled women like Addison. They aren't used to being asked to do physical labor—they think they're above it. But they aren't. And I realized it was my job to teach her as much.

I sprayed her down and then I emptied the overflowing pot. It was horrendous, but I did it. All the while, I explained to her the importance of being clean. Just like my mother and father used to do to me. I gave her a pass this time, my love.

But she would pay for it, William.

Lord, would she pay.

I told her there would be no more water for her until she scrubbed that room squeaky clean. I gave her a toothbrush and bleach just like my father used to give me.

After I'd sprayed her down, I ordered her to remove her clothing, but she just sat there staring, completely still, watching me, just the way my father used to. God, I hated that. This made me angry. Plus, I wanted—no, I *needed* to see her naked. More importantly, I needed the goddamned picture to show the doctor. Only, she refused to remove her clothes. She refused to move at all.

I warned her. I did.

I retrieved my mother's favorite cane and I hit her with it.

And then, I did it again until she turned over and did her pathetic crawl into a ball thing, and so I hit her once more for good measure. That time, I drew blood. I could see it seeping out of the gaping wound just beneath the wet, pale blouse she was wearing, and I wanted to taste it. I wanted to know what she tasted like. I wanted to lick her wounds. I shouldn't have hit her, William. And it was then I realized the problem. She'd gotten the best of me. She'd provoked me and I'd let her. Gah! I couldn't photograph her bloody and bruised. To do so would raise suspicion, and we can't have that—now could we?

I had to think. I had to switch up the game plan and fast. So I retrieved a little something from my bag (my mobile pharmacy, as I like to call it), and I informed her that it was her choice. We could do this dead or alive. And guess what? Immediately, when she saw the syringe, her face changed. I'd beaten her. Both literally *and* metaphorically.

She didn't want the drugs. She didn't want to die.

For a minute, I was happy. Because we still have so much work to do, she and I.

But then, I was mad. She made me draw blood. She made me want to taste her! She ruined my photo opportunity.

Now, I'd have to figure something else out.

For that—she would pay.

And, oh, God, you should have seen her. She acted like she wasn't scared… but I knew the truth! Addison can act all she wants, but I will beat her. I will show her the depth of her fear—of what it means to be truly afraid. It wasn't very nice of her to test me this way. She was supposed to have learned to appreciate all that I'm doing for her—but she hasn't! She defied me, and now she will see what my wrath looks like.

With that thought, I brought down my heel, and I landed it right atop her left kidney. She winced, and then I screamed and kicked her again and again, all the while I said all the things she needed to hear. At last, after a few more kicks, I heard her finally whimper, then I turned and left, and I locked the door behind me.

When I returned, it was with her penance.

From now on, I decided I would treat her like the bitch she is.

She looked directly at me as I placed the canned dog food next to her face. She watched me while I warned her that if it wasn't eaten up by the time I returned, that she'd learn her lesson by way of the drugs.

She didn't respond. But I watched her eyes, and I'm relatively sure she got the message.

Gosh, you know… I really don't know why she has to be so stubborn!

But two can play at this game, my love. Don't worry about that.

Clearly, you must like this sort of thing…

She taught me that about you, and now I will teach her.

She *has* to learn, William. Sooner rather than later, she just has to.

I am the boss now.

And she is my little pet.

Yours truly,

L

~

CHAPTER TWENTY-ONE

Day Twenty

Dear William,

Lydia is back and it is worse than I imagined. I'm tired today and not feeling well, and while I won't write about all of the despicable things she is having me do, I will tell you of one of them.

Lydia wants to become me. She is convinced somehow that she is a caterpillar in the process of becoming a butterfly.

Her words.

At first, I wanted nothing to do with helping Lydia do anything. But after experiencing some of the continued horrors here and considering that there is now a baby on the way (which she does not know about, nor will she), I decided to hear her out on the latest idea. She wants to study me and in order to do so she says she needs photos. All kinds of photos. This is actually good news, I decided in the end. Because here is what I know about photos: The subject needs to be worth photographing. They need to be well taken care of and well fed and well... you get the picture. In addition, the more physical evidence that I am alive and out there, the better. I figure soon enough she has to slip up and maybe, just maybe, one of the photos might end up in hands that will help me get out of here.

Anyway, so she hauls in all of the outfits, and, of course, a pair of black Louboutins, which she said she learned about during my days acting as a Domme. She says she wants to learn to be a Domme herself so that you'll love her all the more. We ended up taking dozens of photos in a ton of different outfits against a white screen. There were so many outfits, it took me back to the days of working at Seven, and it made me think of you. Not all of those memories are bad, of course.

That said, I couldn't imagine what she wants with these photos, but she says she plans to Photoshop them. She showed me a few, and it was hard to believe it was actually me in the photo. I've lost so much weight being here, and I'm sure some of it is also due to the ~~morning~~ all-day sickness I've been having. I do my best to hide this from Lydia, and so far, I think I've done ok. I don't believe she's suspected anything.

Oddly enough, after all of the days I've spent locked away alone, the experience of playing dress up was a rather good one. It was nice to try on clothes and have some actual human interaction. Even if it was with someone as batshit crazy as Lydia. Also, I'm well aware of Stockholm Syndrome. I can assure you this is not the case here. But I did agree to train her to be a Domme as, one, I need to gain her trust. And two, I need to find a way to get physical enough with her that I gain myself a way out of here.

I will fucking kill her, William.

I don't care anymore. I have to get out of here. I feel like I'm losing my mind. This room is so small and the walls are closing in.

I just need to get my strength up and ensure I can make it out before she finds out about the pregnancy. Because, if she finds out, it will be a double strike against me. One, she'll see me as weak. Two, I'll have something she wants. As a bonus, it will be a reminder of our love.

Speaking of the pregnancy, I've been spotting a bit. Nothing major, and I do remember spotting some early on with the boys. Also, Lydia thinks this is my period, which is another reason she likely doesn't suspect anything.

Lastly, I miss the boys so much. It's hard to believe it's been three weeks now since I've seen their faces. I'm trying to stay positive, I really am—but I just miss you guys so much and I'm so very tired. I'm not even sure that any of what I'm writing makes any sense so, for now, I am going to wrap it up and try to get some sleep.

There is a tiny bit of light that manages to come through a crack in the outside wall and some nights, the moon shines through. I look at the soft light, and I wonder if you might be, too. I know it's a silly thing, but thinking that you are, brings me hope that soon we'll be together again.

Love,
Addison

❧

Day Twenty-Five

Dear William,

Lydia is gone again. She says she will be away for three days and has left me enough food and water to make it through.

Today, I am angry. I am angry that I am in this dark, muggy room, made of wood and covered in dirt.

I am angry you are out there and I am angry about the events that led me to be in this position. You shouldn't have lied to me. Today, I wonder if this had not happened whether or not our marriage would have survived. It's easy, now, being here with my life on the line, to minimize the problems we had but, the truth is, since I'm locked in here alone—in part because you were being stalked and refused to discuss it (among other things) with me. And the thing is, I have nothing *but* time to think these things over.

I want to believe that we could've and still can make it. What I know is that I love you. But is love enough? I don't know.

I don't know why I went from one day being the woman who gave you what you need to suddenly being your wife whose role you so clearly had defined that you never even bothered to ask whether or not the role fit what I had in mind.

And somehow, the loneliness that comes with being locked in this fucking room makes me remember how it felt to be alone in our marriage. I sit here and I wonder what my part was in that. Did I love you enough? Did I focus too much on the kids? Did I deny you what you needed?

I don't know.

What I do know, though, is that you are the kind of man you are. You're an alpha in every sense of the word, and a part of that person is the man I fell in love with. But there's this other side, too. The side I question whether or not is compatible with an actual partnership. Because that's what a marriage is.

And I'm just not certain, no matter how much the two of us love each other, that you'll ever be the kind of man who's okay with being half of a whole.

Which is too bad. I never wanted you to be just one more someone in my life who wanted me to be something I couldn't.

And the worst part is… that when I look back at the events that took place over the past few months, I'm almost certain you feel the same.

Love,

Addison

~

Day Twenty-Eight

Dear William,

I'm less angry today. It's astonishing the difference a few days make. I blame the hormones. It's nice to be able to write it all out. But I do question what would happen if I don't make it out of here. How would that letter make you feel? Not good, I suspect. So it's just one more thing to keep me going. Don't die, I tell myself. Otherwise, that will be the last letter from you he reads. I know it sounds silly but you'd be surprised the lengths I go to, to keep myself from going crazy.

Today I am scared. It is hot, the flies are swarming, and I am covered in mosquito bites. I do not believe I am that far from the coast—given the weather and the bugs.

Speaking of the coast, oh, what I wouldn't give to see the outdoors. To feel just a bit of fresh air upon my skin. It's so very dark in here as it's rained for days now.

Lydia hasn't returned, and I haven't been able to hold anything other than water down for at least the past twenty-four hours. It's gotten so bad that I am weak and too dizzy to sit up.

I don't know if I can make it through this. I really don't.

I need to go to a hospital.

When Lydia returns (and God I hope it's soon), I'm going to tell her about the baby. I'm going to tell her that I need to see a doctor.

I'll promise that she can have the baby. That's what she'll want. At this point, I will do and give her whatever she wants. Or at least, I'll let her think I will.

Because if she doesn't take me, I'm not sure it will matter anyhow.

If any of these letters ever make their way to you, please know that I tried. I tried so hard.

I love you. I've loved you with everything I've ever had.

I've also written letters to the boys. You will find them tucked behind this one.

I love you. Please take care of the boys for me. See to it that Patrick does right by them. I hope you'll stay in their lives and that you will find love again.

Perhaps, I will end up just a short story in a long collection of yours. While for me, you and my children were the whole of my story. You were everything. And I am okay with that.

I have no doubt you will be fine. You will do well in life, William.

You always have.

Love,

Addison

❦

CHAPTER TWENTY-TWO

Day Twenty-Eight

WILLIAM HAD ASKED SONDRA TO MEET HIM AT SEVEN. HE needed to see Addison's office. He'd been there, but only once, after searching her primary office back at the agency. He couldn't help but think there was something there, something he was missing, hidden in the studio. As Addison's assistant, and Scott Hammons' daughter, certainly Lydia had to have known about his wife's prior work at the 'dungeon.' Also, visiting gave him a chance to speak with Sondra. To his credit, he hadn't seen her since he'd learned his wife was officially missing. But that didn't mean there wasn't a part of him that wanted to.

"This seems pointless," William said, shaking his head.

"Just talk," Sondra urged him once again. "Let it out."

William walked around the small office his wife once occupied. He could still smell her when he sat down behind her desk. "What's there to say?"

Sondra tilted her head. She glared at him. "You do want to find your wife, don't you?"

William dropped the pen he'd lifted from the desk and did a double take. "What kind of question is that?"

"An honest one."

"Of course, I want to find her."

"Well, then," Sondra said, motioning toward him. "Let's hear it."

"You see," he said. "That's what I mean. It would be one thing if she were going to hear me out. But she isn't."

"It'll be good for you to get it off of your chest."

William's jaw set.

"What would you say to her if she were here right now?"

"I'd say that the chances of that are relatively slim. Because she isn't here. I shouldn't be here, either..."

"Then why'd you come?"

William could hear the bitterness in her voice. "I wanted to see if she had anything here—something I may have missed."

"That isn't what I'm looking for," she said shaking her head. "How are you feeling?"

"Like I should be out there doing something," he replied pointing toward the door. "Like I should be trying to find the crazy bitch responsible for her disappearance. Like— talking about my feelings with you isn't going to get the job done."

"You are doing something. You're here."

He scoffed.

"William," Sondra huffed. "I can see that you aren't sleeping. You look like hell," she added, twisting her mouth. "Just get it out. What's going on with you?"

"What do you think is going on? I miss her."

"Tell me about it."

"Fine," he relented eventually. "It's just... well, there are so many things I should have told her. Before." He paused and then he looked away. "*Before.* That sounds so strange to say aloud."

"Strange how?"

"Strange as in—it's not as though there's some measure of time that has made everything different."

She furrowed her brow. "Isn't it different, though?"

"She's gone. That's different. I don't know what to do about it. That's not."

"Any new leads?" Sondra asked trying to sound hopeful.

William shook his head solemnly. "No," he said. "And what's worse is… the cops think I'm at fault in her disappearance," he added with a heavy sigh.

"Yes," she said. "But we knew that. *Everyone* knows that."

"My point exactly."

"That must feel pretty bad."

He nodded. "I've given them everything. I've handed over the letters Lydia Hammons wrote saying she is holding her captive somewhere. I don't know what else to do."

"And?"

"They have nothing on me, their hands are just as tied as mine are. They talk a big game but they're not putting their all into finding her—because they already believe I'm guilty of something sinister."

"But you're not."

He threw up his hands. "That's beside the point. The Feds —they're incompetent, and I feel powerless as to what to do about it."

"Powerless…huh…"

He raised his brow. "I bet that's something you never thought you'd hear me say—"

"Do you really believe that?"

William shook his head. "No. I mean—I may *feel* powerless—but I'm not. It's just… I've thrown every resource I have into bringing her back home safely. In fact, when I leave here

I'm hopping on the heli to fly down to the bay. There's a search party going out."

"That's something."

He shrugged. "Her face is plastered everywhere."

"Tell me about it."

"But it's not enough," he said. "None of it is enough. It hurts. It hurts and I don't even know where to begin to deal with the pain. So, instead, I search."

"You haven't been *here*. I mean… you haven't needed a session. That's good news."

"Needed isn't exactly accurate," he assured her. "I've just been too busy poring over maps, combing over the details of details, looking over any and every shred of evidence—anything that could lead to the possibility of figuring out where she might be."

"I can see that you aren't sleeping."

He shifted. "I know she's out there and that she's alive. My heart knows it. That and I simply refuse to believe there is any other outcome other than finding her and bringing her home safe."

Sondra pressed her lips to one another. "And the boys? How are the boys holding up?"

"They're doing as well as can be expected. I've flown in several leading child psychologists—even though, personally, I think psychologists are full of shit—but that is what was recommended, and well, she might be happy to know that I've finally started listening." William half-smiled. "I will stop at nothing to see that they are taken care of."

"So, not so powerless after all."

He pressed his lips to one another. "Who's to say?"

~

Day Thirty

WILLIAM WATCHED THE INK SPILL ONTO THE PAGE. HE'D BEEN advised to talk to the shrink he'd hired for the boys and even though he hated shrinks, he was assured it would help bring his wife home as well as lessen the pain in their eyes, then who was he to refuse? It was the shrink who'd advised that the entire family write to Addison. It would help process the emotions the children were feeling around the sudden disappearance of their mother. William didn't agree. He thought it would be too painful. Another admission that she might not be coming back. But he hadn't said as much. At least not in front of the children. He'd let Patrick decide what was best. Which is why it surprised even him when he found himself writing to her in the wee hours of the morning.

Dear Addison,

Never in a million years since the day you found your way back to me after the 'Patrick debacle' did I ever think I could go thirty days without seeing your face or hearing your voice.

And yet here we are.

The search hasn't turned up much, and it would be easy to lose hope, just as it seems the cops are doing. They say the case remains open and active, but I don't see much happening there.

Thankfully, I have the resources to continue on my own in spite of their inefficiency. We are looking. I want to assure you of that. And maybe myself, too, because it never seems like I'm doing enough. I sleep two to three hours a night (if that), but otherwise, I am working with the team of experts we have put in place to find you. I've brought in the best of the best, and I do believe we are making progress even though to me—one more day that you are out there and not here with your children and me—hardly feels like progress. It feels like torture.

Speaking of torture, I want to apologize, Addison. I am sorry for so many things, one of those things being the fact that I lied to you. Worse, I shut you out. I should have asked for your help sooner. I should have communicated with you. Hindsight is twenty-twenty, I suppose.

I realize now that I suffer from PTSD. Or—at least that's what the shrinks say anyway. You know me—I hate shrinks and I hate labels, but the thing is that sadly, your absence gave me something to fight for. In order to give my all to finding you, I knew it meant I had to get help. I only wish it hadn't come to this. I have taken up an hour of martial arts several times a week (for real, it's not a cover this time). Although, ironically enough, I hardly have the focus nor the energy with you missing and all that is happening with the investigation. Usually, I just sort of get beat to hell. But at least I am not seeking services from Sondra, I guess.

I've taken a leave of absence from my companies, and although there are still a few projects I'm involved with—my workload is fairly minimal as these days my primary focus is on finding you. I'm seeing a shrink twice a week, which I admittedly do not like. However, of all the shrinks, I've found one I can almost tolerate. And while I still refuse medication to deal with the PTSD, we are trying some other therapies, and I guess you could say they are going as well as can be expected.

But the truth is, nothing is going very well here without you. However, while it may not seem like it, in the grand scheme of things, the shrink assures me this is progress. He says it's a good thing I've found myself attached to someone who I can't live without. He assures me this is a good sign, a step toward recovery. Recovery of what? I don't know. I'm trying hard to share his sentiment.

Because if I'm being honest (and isn't that the whole point?) you're still missing, and here I am, attached—and it hurts like hell.

All my love,

William

≈

CHAPTER TWENTY-THREE

Thirty-Five Days Missing (Her)
Eighteen Days Free (Me)

Dearest William,

I just realized I never told you how I did it. I never told you how I captured your wife, did I?

My bad. Allow me…

Addison, being the whiny diva that she is, seemed to be having a hard time about some 'personal issues.'

Which I took to mean that you'd finally come to see the light and were ready to admit our love for one another. I knew it was just a matter of time!

Anyway, she was all mopey on that particular day, so I suggested we go and find ice cream and then do a little shopping. Retail therapy seems to be girls like Addison's M.O. I'll never understand how a new 'one more thing you really don't need' can make someone feel better about themselves when really it's just another shitty choice in a long line of them, but I digress. It's useless to try to understand the idiocy of women like her. On the first three attempts of getting her away from that house, I was shot down. On the fourth, I was met with hesitance. On the fifth, she was grabbing her bag and walking to my car. You see, William, this is why you *never* give up!

So, we start driving and I ask her if she wants coffee, and Addison, being the spoiled person that she is, of course, wants coffee at 3 PM. Of course, she does. Why anyone needs to pay six bucks for a lousy cup of joe when they could self-medicate with much higher quality stuff via the pharmaceutical route, I'll also never understand. But I go in and order the coffee and just to prove my point, I slip in a little something extra—a pretty potent well-known sleeping aid. About forty-five minutes later, she's out! I keep driving, and when we get to our destination, I realized that, uh-oh, maybe I hadn't planned this so well. I couldn't rouse her. No matter what I did, I couldn't get her up. So I did what I had to do, and I fetched an old half-broken wheelbarrow—only, trouble was, I couldn't get her into it.

And then it hit me. I was either going to have to drag her or I was going to have to get help.

You will be happy to know that I went with option two.

Which leads to my latest 'situation.'

After I had managed to shuffle her back into the seat, I drove into the nearest small town. I waltzed into a run-down hardware shop just before closing. My luck! I tell ya. Anywho, I located one of the little worker boys, well, actually... he was the *only* worker boy. He happened to be hauling trash out to the dumpster around back when I spotted him and called him over. Then, I showed him my 'sister' in the backseat who was 'sick' and told him we were staying just up the road. I asked him if he would mind helping me get her into the house, told him I'd pay him twenty bucks for the trouble. When he appeared a bit hesitant and said his ride would be waiting, I doubled the offer and told him I'd drive him home as well. See! Persistence. I watched an interview with you once on YouTube and that was what you said. You said, persistence pays. You probably don't remember, but I hope you know that I took it to heart. Not to spoil the ending for you or anything but... of course, the kid said yes. As it turns out, thankfully, on the way back to our 'place,' I found out he's actually not so young after all, and at nineteen, he's already had a few run-ins with the law. Mostly petty stuff like trespassing, but one never can be too careful you know. He told me his story, and I told him, pointing to the back seat, that my sister had cancer and that I was taking her out to our 'country home' so she could go in peace. He seemed kind of sad by that, but he just shrugged and offered nothing particularly

176

profound. I guess I wasn't completely lying. Addison may not actually have cancer. She IS a cancer!

Anyway…so, we get to the place, and I'll admit it is kind of a dump. He assists me by helping me carry her in. I took her hands, he took her feet, and it's all fine and well until he sees the room. He eyes the padlocks and I can tell by his expression, he isn't the kind of smart that just lets this sort of thing go. I mean, he tries. He stutters and he stammers when he sees the gun—but I know his type. I aim it at him and he throws his hands up and says, "Whoa lady. You ain't gotta worry 'bout me. I won't tell no one." He had this expression like, you know, he sees this kind of thing all the time, but I wasn't buying it. I ordered him out of the house and down to the storm cellar. Lo' and behold the sneaky little bastard tried to make a run for it, so I took a shot at his knee cap, but only managed to get his foot. I'd say it's more of a surface wound than anything, but he got the point. He didn't try to run again, it would have been tough anyhow, with all that blood filling his shoe. You should have seen his face though. He begged me not to put him in the cellar, but what was I supposed to do? In he went, and the good news is, you can't hear a thing down there. In fact, I almost forgot about the poor bastard. But then, I remembered I might need him when and if it comes time to do some heavy lifting.

And you know the weird thing is… I went back to that hardware store a few days later to get some cable ties, and I asked after him and the manager said he'd moved on. He complained about the little shit not showing up for work, and then he said it was probably for the best. That's the funny thing, sometimes, my love, people can vanish, and no one misses them. What a sad existence, really. It makes me think I've kind of done this kid a favor, don't you? If not him, then for sure his boss. Saved him the headache of firing him, he'd said.

I honestly thought he would've croaked in my absence when I was locked up, but somehow the little bastard made it. Says he survived on cockroaches and rainwater. How's that for crazy? Now, the trouble is… whenever I go down, he whines a lot, and I think his foot is infected. I mean, sure, I don't give him much in the way of food, and he's dropped a lot of weight, and it shouldn't be too long now… but I don't know—he's sort of just taking up space, ya know what I mean? That's an interesting topic, too… there are a lot of people in this world, William, who exist just to take up space. They expect everything to be handed to them and claim they have 'rights.' At the same time, they offer no real contribution and quite frankly, I'm sick of people like that. No one has a 'right' to a hot meal or a warm bed or… anything, really. These things have to be earned. Just like my parents taught me. Even here under lock and key, Addison, and that kid, they both think they're entitled to something. Well, that stops now! They are going to have to learn what it means to earn even the simplest of things in this world. Just like you and I had to. That's why they are here. There's a method to my madness. They deserve to be taught a lesson. And sometimes, just as my parents taught me, lessons have to be learned the hard way. All of the people I've ever hurt were bottom feeders, entitled fuckers who insisted on learning the hard way. They were people who offered no real value to the world which is why they have been hardly missed. But you and I, my dear, are *not* those kind of people.

And, my gosh, how I wish you were here to help me figure out what to do with this bag of bones on my hands. I'm sure you would come up with something smart for the kid—something other than just letting him slowly rot.

It almost just seems too easy.

Yours truly,

L

~

Thirty-Six Days Missing (Her)
Nineteen Days Free (Me)

Dearest William,

So I've been thinking about you a lot. It's been really getting to me, us being apart.

And that's when I realized that maybe the kid does have a purpose.

Or two.

One, I need to get laid.

Two, I need your wife to teach me to be a Dominatrix.

Three, oh, did I mention there was a third thing?

No, well—I just figured it out.

Three, your wife needs to toughen up. She needs to see the pain she inflicts on others.

She needs to be taught that what she's done is *not* okay.

I think the kid shall be that lesson.

Love you always and forever,

L

P.S. Another poem for you:

He takes my hand in his and

the warmth of him envelopes me.

It was just a handshake.

But I felt it then.

And it wasn't nothing.

~

Thirty-Seven Days Missing (Her)
Twenty Days Free (Me)

Dearest William,

I introduced Addison to the kid. You should have seen her face! Her eyeballs nearly leapt out of her head and then she wept. She actually wept. Serves her right for all of the trouble she's been giving me lately. I should tell you about her demands. The latest was vitamins. She wanted vitamins. Vitamins! Can you believe it? After all I'm doing for her and she asks for a silly little thing like vitamins.

Truth be told, the boy is in bad shape. His foot is overrun with pus and infection, and he's feverish. He likely doesn't weigh more than seventy-five pounds give or take a few, his eyes are sunken, and I practically had to drag him from the storm cellar to the house. He can't really stand, and it's kind of a shame as it seems to have decided his own fate.

You see, before I hauled him up to the house, I thought we might have a little fun. I thought he might like to touch a woman one last time, and you know... be touched. But no, he couldn't perform. He told me I was sick. What kind of man says that when a woman offers sex? I don't know. And for that, he had to pay. Once I got him back to the house, I brought out my hammer, and I had Addison use it on that ol' foot of his. She didn't want to. Really, she didn't. She wept and she vomited, but then I got the gun and I put it to the kid's temple and that's when she finally started to take me seriously.

I willed her to call my bluff. I willed her not to bring that hammer down on his foot. I would have shot him, and it wouldn't have even mattered. It would have made things easy. The truth is he's probably going to die within the next day or two anyway, only now the blood is going to be on her hands.

She begged me to take him to the hospital, but I told her he was her problem now. When she hit him, you should have seen the blood and pus splatter. It was quite artistic, the pattern it made on the walls.

At least now, things don't look so drab.

She vomited. The kid passed out. Then she begged some more.

She likes to bargain, that one.

And I have to say, it feels really good to be needed.

Yours,

L

P.S. I wrote you a poem. It is reminiscent of our time together in Italy…

That's How You Know.

I remember it so clearly.

That night.

With stars in your eyes

I remember.

The sound of your voice

and the way it shook

ever so slightly

as the words slipped off your tongue.

"I'm nervous," you whispered.

As I watched the moonlight dance across your skin.

BEYOND BEDROCK

I remember.

That I knew I loved you then.

I didn't say so—

I simply smiled and said,

"That's how you know it matters."

And it was enough.

You sighed

looked up at the sky

then back at me.

I knew the stars would keep our secrets.

And they have.

∼

CHAPTER TWENTY-FOUR

Day Sixty-Eight

Dear William,

Lydia is growing more unstable by the day. One minute she's manic, she'll be on a high I've never seen before, and then she goes low. Very low. It's hard to judge her moods and now she is gone again for another surgery. She doesn't say that's where she's going, but she's always gone for two to three days and then comes back bandaged up. She mentioned once that she's getting medication from Mexico, and I believe that's where she goes for her surgeries, too.

I haven't written as much because I've been pretty busy. I don't know why I never assumed that if Lydia were holding me here that there might be others as well, but the truth is I never gave it much thought.

Then, about a month ago, she brings in a boy. A boy who was very near death. I've helped him recover some, and I think that he just might make it. His name is Bryan, and he is nineteen and is originally from Dallas. He tells me that we're in a rural area outside of Elsa, Texas. He says he remembers driving west for about thirty minutes or so away from Elsa, but he hadn't paid much attention to the signs or roads, so he couldn't be quite sure of our exact location. We're making a plan to escape. With his strength building a little more each day, and my pregnancy getting to the point where I won't be able to hide it much longer, we believe that we can overpower Lydia and make it out of here.

It won't be easy. I am still chained at the ankle and Bryan's hands are zip-tied. I didn't write for a while because, to be honest, I wasn't sure I could trust him. I still haven't told him outright about the baby. Speaking of which, the all-day sickness has started to subside a little. I never quite wrote about how I've hidden all of the vomit from Lydia... Well, in the corner of the room there is a place where the floorboard is missing. Underneath appears to be a crawl space or maybe it's just poor building, I don't know. About two feet down, it's just soil and I dug a little hole there. That's where I'd throw up and cover it afterward. It's pretty disgusting, but it helped, especially when it happened several times per day.

As Bryan has grown less frail and has started to become more and more lucid, one day out of the blue, he asked why I buried my throw up. I told him it was for hygiene and also so that Lydia didn't know she was getting to me. I can only assume that a nineteen-year-old boy has little experience with morning sickness, because he didn't press further. Then, a few days later, he casually mentioned with as much digging as I do every day, that I probably could have dug the both of us out of here by now, and that's when it hit me that perhaps he was right. Maybe it was a viable option—maybe I could dig underneath the cabin and get us out of here.

Bryan's hands are (literally) tied so he can't do a lot in the way of digging. But he does seem fairly knowledgeable where construction is concerned. He estimates I can have us out of here in a matter of a month or two—maybe sooner the more Lydia stays gone. Hopefully, though, we'll have already been found by then.

Lydia assures me they've called off the search. Knowing you, I don't believe that for a minute.

I miss you and the boys so much, and I think of you every single day.

It is nice to have some company in here.

This and the baby keep me going.

Love,

Addison

≈

Month Four

Dear William,

I don't think I've told you much about Lydia's transformation. These days, she's looking an awful lot like the old me. It's scary and a bit eerie to see, to be honest. Sometimes, when she comes in, which hasn't been often lately other than to deliver food and water, I have to do a double take because the resemblance to who I used to be is so striking.

The time came recently where I began marking things in terms of months instead of days, and that is perhaps one of the saddest realizations I've had since being here. What I thought would be hours, turned into days and then weeks and now months. I can hardly stand to think about what comes after that. I have started to show a little. I finally told Bryan about the baby yesterday. It felt so good just to say it aloud. He seemed genuinely concerned, but not all that surprised. He says he has lots of brothers and sisters and he's seen 'this kind of thing' a time or two.

I've still managed to keep the news from Lydia, and I've made significant progress with the digging over the past few days. Once I got past all of the vomit, it wasn't so bad. But it is draftier in here now, and damp. I'm afraid Lydia might notice, so when she comes in, I distract her to the best of my ability. In fact, Bryan and I often play good cop, bad cop. She wanted me to train her to become a Dominatrix and so we use Bryan as our submissive. When we 'play,' as she calls it, we get to go out into the living area. She detaches my chain and re-attaches it to a spike in there. She binds Bryan's hands and feet as well as blindfolds him. I've looked around the cabin (which is putting it nicely—it's more of a shack, really) to try to find a way out, but the door is padlocked from the inside, and I've yet to see a set of keys lying around. There is only one window from what I have seen and it is boarded up. There's a small kitchen with a wood-burning stove, a small sink. We don't have power, but Lydia has flashlights, and honestly, it's usually so dark in our room that I don't notice anyway. That tiny crack in the wall in our room is the only light we see and when the sun is shining, it is magnificent. It's just a crack. But at least it's something. It's early fall now and just starting to cool down. I sometimes wonder what winter might be like without heat, but I made it through the dreadful summer heat, so I figure it can't be that bad. And yet, I try not to think too hard about it because I don't plan to be around here in the winter. I plan to be home with you and my children.

Speaking of children, it has been a blessing that I have been able to keep Bryan alive. Whenever Lydia looks at him, I can tell he is disposable and I can see that he recognizes it, too. He often plays sicker than he really is, and when I am forced to do my part on him during 'play time,' I always land the blows just right so they won't hurt as much. I've also delayed showing her anything extreme. So far. Bryan says it isn't too bad—although I am not sure I believe him. Sometimes, I hear him crying at night and I can relate. This is when it gets to me, too. But I stare at the hole, and I know that I am one day closer to seeing you and the boys and that makes all the difference.

I don't think Bryan has that, which makes me both sad and scared for him at the same time.

Love,

Addison

~

Month Five

Dear William,

I felt the baby move for the first time today. The first 'real' kick—the kind you can't mistake for anything other than what it is.

And it was every bit as breathtaking as I remember it to be.

I can't believe it sometimes still.

There is life inside of me and it is ours.

Love,

Addison

~

Month Six

Dear William,

Lydia found out about the baby today. It was time for my monthly shower and what happened was this—for four months, I managed to hide it. Not today, though.

Anyway, she led me to the shower and ordered me to undress, and as I did, I realized what was going to happen. There was no hiding it anymore. I tried to distract her with talk of the latest Domme training we'd been working on, but she just had this focused look on her face as though she finally realized something she'd known for a long while. Then her face lit up and the biggest smile I'd ever seen overtook it. "You whore," she said. "You dirty little whore."

I stood there puzzled waiting to be let out of the cold water and half wanting to stay in. "I knew all along you were fucking him," she said. "I knew it!"

I stared at her and for the briefest of moments, considering my options. I considered letting her think the baby was indeed Bryan's, but in the end, I couldn't do it. I knew that I'd be safer if she knew the truth.

"The baby is William's, Lydia," I told her. "Do the math."

She considered my statement as the smile faded slowly, and then all at once, she lost it. For a second, she tore at me, clawing at my skin, and I was trapped. I wriggled and ducked, but I was tied to the chain on the edge of the tub and there was little I could do to get out in front of her. I figured I was going to die and that's when I heard it. Bryan was screaming at the top of his lungs. They were the most deafening screams I'd ever heard. And as long as I live, I don't think that's a sound I'll ever forget. All of a sudden, Lydia stopped, and she turned and exited the bathroom as I sat clutching my stomach.

She was gone for quite some time as I sat there on the cold, hard tile shivering.

When she returned, her expression had changed and her whole demeanor was different. She was humming.

She tossed a towel in my direction. "Your roomie had an unfortunate accident. But it seems he'll be okay."

"What kind of accident?"

"Jesus, Addison. How many different kinds do you think there are?"

I didn't answer.

"Bryan's weak," she quipped. "He tried to off himself by tightening the ties around his neck. No worries, though. Unfortunately, for all of us, he survived." She said it so nonchalantly as though she were describing the weather.

I gripped the worn towel a little tighter as my belly tightened, and I prayed to someone, anyone to let it be okay. And by it, I meant the baby and Bryan and myself...

Lydia yanked on the chain urging me to rise to my feet. "I suppose this only means one thing..."

She waited, but I didn't respond. I simply glared at her.

"I'm going to have to start feeding you better," she said with a sigh. "William would never approve of our child being treated this way."

Her child. Yes. Of course. I could have corrected her, the way I did before.

But instead, I let her believe.

We are all safer that way.

Love,

Addison

~

CHAPTER TWENTY-FIVE

Day 182

Dear Addison,

I started these letters to you in hopes it would help ease the pain of your absence, and although I can't say that it has, I can say that I at least have a daily journal of all that has happened since you've been away. I've chronicled the search and I've written in detail things the boys have done or said. I've written about soccer games and holidays—and everything in between because it helps to feel that, in some way, you are closer, but also, so that when you come home, you will be able to read for yourself all that has taken place. We are closer today than ever.

We have reason to believe you may have crossed the border into Mexico.

I am on South Padre Island again speaking to anyone and everyone who may have seen someone resembling you or Lydia.

Jess is in a small town just north of me, and I am told that Sondra is taking on another rural town just west of where Jess is.

The boys are doing well. We talk about you every day, and we've made sure to include them in the search as much as possible.

I love and miss you.

Love,

William

Lost count of the days. (Me)
As they say, time flies when you're having fun. (Her)

Dearest William,

Things have been pretty hectic around here.

You have no idea.

For one, we are going to have a baby! A BABY! Can you believe it?

I'm just so thrilled! Today, I wear red in honor of my excitement. I just knew all of this trouble with Addison wouldn't be in vain. You see, I wanted to get rid of her months ago, but I figured since she'd managed to nab you—to trick you into falling in love with her, that I had better take some time and try to figure her out.

Plus, there was always another plan. But you probably know that one by now. You see, I've been crossing the border, and these days, now that I'm looking more and more like Addison, they're starting to get suspicious, I can tell. This last time, when I produced my fake ID, they studied it just a second longer.

I know you're searching and I know you're getting close.

Just a little longer now.

And we will be together.

We will be a family.

Yours always,

L

Month Six

Dear William,

Something terrible has happened.

Bryan and I made a pact. We had a plan. The plan went horribly wrong.

What was supposed to have happened was that during our next Domme session, we decided it was 'go time.' We would have to take Lydia.

My role was to show Lydia how to flip a submissive in the event that something went wrong, and she needed to regain control of the situation quickly. Bryan's part was just to get his hands on Lydia. He was supposed to place his zip-tied hands around her neck, and I was to handle the rest from there. Bryan did his job. He put his hands around her neck and I saw her smile. And then it all happened so fast. I saw something in his eyes flicker. Recognition, maybe. Lydia turned to face him slowly and deliberately. As though this was the way it was supposed to happen all along. Bryan looked over her shoulder back at me, and he frowned. I called out to Lydia. I tried. I tried so hard to get her attention, but everything happened so fast. I saw Bryan's face go slack and then all the color drained. He wore an expression of defeat and then something else. A small smile, if I'm not mistaken. That's when Lydia pulled back and I saw it. There was blood. So much blood.

"Fuck flipping," she laughed. "You see… that's how this is done, Addison. There's no playing around when it comes to one's safety." She stepped backward and turned to face me. "*You* of all people should know that," she added.

I went to Bryan and placed my hand over his wound to stop the blood. He slumped, and I called his name over and over. I'll never forget the look on his face. He just stared straight ahead. His eyes glossy, his jaw slack.

"You remove that knife, and he's a goner," she warned. "It's the only thing keeping him from bleeding out."

"He *is* bleeding out," I screamed. "You stabbed him twice. In the stomach. We have to get help," I said. I begged.

Lydia watched me for a moment and then quietly sat down on the floor as though nothing at all was amiss. She told me of her father and of some of the horrible things he had done. That's when she let me in on the fact that her father was Scott Hammons. I wasn't surprised, I told her. I wanted to be. But I wasn't.

She smiled and then she began to rock back and forth, back and forth while repeating over and over, "Thy will be done. Thy will be done. Thy will be done." She wasn't serious though. She was toying with me.

All the while, I held my hand over Bryan's stomach and pled with her to call for help.

Eventually, she stood and dusted herself off. She told me it was all my fault. She said that I'd have to be punished and then she left.

She just fucking left, William.

It's been almost three days, and now I am here locked in this room with Bryan's dead body.

I have to get out.

So, I'm going to try the hole. I don't think it's ready but—

There's simply no other choice.

I'm next.

No matter what happens, I pray you get my letters and you know that I love you.

Please tell the boys that I love them so very much.

Love,

Addison

～

CHAPTER TWENTY-SIX

Addison spent forty-nine hours trapped in that hole before Lydia found her. The hole had ultimately been too narrow for her burgeoning belly and it had taken her a full day to make it to her final resting place, at which point, she realized she could go no further. No matter how hard she tried, she couldn't move forward and yet she couldn't make herself go back, either, so long as the cuff and chain were firmly attached to her ankle. She'd stretched the chain as far as it would go and while she kicked and struggled against it, ripping flesh from her ankle in the process, it held. She'd dug hard, ripped her fingernails off, and wore the pads of her fingers down to nothing in an attempt to get through what remained of the hole. Stuck, it seemed her only option was to use the fishing knife she'd pulled from Bryan's innards to cut off her foot. She willed herself to do it, and she would have if only she could have reached it, and also if she hadn't been so afraid that she'd bleed out and die there in the hole—just four feet shy of freedom.

She screamed for help until her voice gave out. She pushed herself and felt the skin around her ankle peel and slide off. She felt the cuff of metal rub against bone and she realized that she was done. It was over, she thought as she lay there looking up at the faintest bit of light. She kept staring until she could just make out the blurry edge of life above ground. She had finally seen daylight and could smell the freshness of the clean air. For the first time in six months. For the first time, after spending the better part of three days locked in a room with a corpse. To say that Addison was in shock would have been an understatement.

She stayed in that position staring at the faint blue sky, dozing on and off until she heard a familiar sound that she knew could only be gravel crunching beneath tires. She pled with whatever God might be listening for it to be anyone but Lydia.

Unfortunately, her prayers went unanswered.

Addison didn't give herself up. She stuffed the knife between her bra and her rib cage, and she let Lydia search for her. Eventually, after ripping up floorboards and discovering the letters in the process, she found Addison trapped in that small hole, beneath the cabin, beneath the earth.

She called out to her. "I know you're down there, you little bitch," she said. "I can hear you breathing."

Shit. Addison needed help she didn't want to need.

"These are some really fancy letters, you know," she chuckled. "You're a real good liar—the way you make me out to be..."

Lydia cackled. Addison heard footsteps on the plywood above. She held her breath. *She's going to shoot.* Addison braced herself. She heard Lydia pull the piece of wood back and fling it aside. "You little witch," she called. "A regular Mrs. Fix it, aren't you?" Addison felt the pull of the chain release and listened as Lydia pulled on it. She twisted the cuff, knowing it would have to remain. Now freed from the constraint of the chain that had held her in place, she struggled to get to the surface where the ground and cabin met, but it was no use.

"I tell you what…" Lydia laughed. "I'm going to be up here reading your magnum opus while you figure out how to get yourself out of there. Don't you worry, though…" she added tauntingly. "I'll be waiting."

Addison tried, but she couldn't move. Some time later, hours later, she heard Lydia retreat and return. Addison felt the vibration of the shovel digging into the earth. "If you aren't coming out, then I guess I'll just have to dig you out. You see, Addison. THIS IS WHAT YOU DO!" she screamed. "Always getting yourself in a bind and expecting someone else to fix it."

Addison waited. Soon enough, she found herself face to face with Lydia's shovel and then a face that closely resembled her own.

When Lydia reached her and saw the way Addison had been tucked into that hole covered in dirt, she slapped her thigh, dropped the shovel, and doubled over. She cackled loudly, placing her hands on her knees. After a few seconds, she rose suddenly as Addison watched something other than amusement flicker across her face. Lydia began frantically digging all the while shouting at Addison about killing *her* baby.

When she'd swept enough dirt away, she reached down and pulled Addison from the hole like a mother yanking on an ill-behaved child. Once she'd gotten her freed completely, she pulled her up from the dirt by her hair and began forcing her back toward the front door.

Addison kicked. She tried twisting her body to no avail. The chain dragged along behind her.

Lydia stopped. "What is that sound?" She turned and eyed the chain and then she let Addison go. She swiftly walked back over to the shovel, picked it up, and walked back to

Addison, who had scooted several feet away. Addison watched in horror as she brought it over her head.

"Noooo!" Addison screamed ducking and covering.

She felt the shovel come down next to her ear with a thud.

Addison slowly uncovered her head.

"Silly. Did you think I was going to hit you?" Lydia asked, her tone flat.

Addison swallowed and scooted backward. She wasn't fast enough, though. After being in that hole for several days, she was in no shape to match Lydia's fury.

"Of course, I'm not going to hit you," she said, shaking her head. "I have something even better planned. It's time to get my baby out."

The baby was healthy enough to survive on its own, Lydia told her. A cesarean section was imminent.

That's when Addison decided. No matter what happened, she was *not* going back in that house. She wouldn't allow herself to be taken back inside. Even if she died in the process, she was not setting foot back inside that cabin. For she knew if she did, she would certainly never make it out alive.

Lydia went for her hair once more. Addison allowed her to grab a fistful as she pulled the knife from her t-shirt. Then she reared back as far as she could go and jammed it into Lydia's thigh. Lydia yanked at her hair harder causing her neck to twist. Still, Addison managed to pull the knife out and stab again and again until Lydia finally let go of her hair and dropped down on top of her.

After several seconds, Lydia covered her and placed her hands around Addison's throat. Addison rammed the knife into whatever flesh she could. She hit bone and still, she pulled back and she stabbed again. She pushed in harder and backed out. Over and over. Eventually, Lydia went slack, the squeezing stopped, and she let go. Addison managed to shove her off and just as soon as she caught her breath, she forced herself upright, stood, and ran for it. Not that running was really an option in her state. Mostly, she stumbled. Still, she did the best she could to put as much distance as she could between the two of them.

When she turned back and saw Lydia sit up, then rise, and stagger forward. *She wasn't dead.* Addison kept running. She didn't look back and she didn't slow down, even though her lungs were seizing up on her. She forced herself to jog onward, one foot in front of the other. She kept going until she reached the road where she stopped just long enough to bend over and attempt to catch her breath. *Keep going, she told herself.*

Wiping the sweat from her forehead, she straightened up. She held her breath and then slowly let it out. She inhaled sharply. Yet, no matter how hard she tried, she couldn't seem to suck in enough air. She glanced from side to side and tried to determine which way to go. She needed to keep moving or she feared she would pass out. *Left or right? Right. No left.* Finally, she turned left.

As she rounded the fence post, she noticed the way the glaring sun beat down on the asphalt. She grew dizzy, stumbled forward and nearly fell. That's when she noticed how bloody her bare feet were. *Was it her blood? Lydia's?* She wanted to glance back, but she wouldn't allow herself to stop long enough to do so. She stammered onward. Her head throbbed. The light was intense, blinding. One hundred or so yards later, she stopped, pausing just long enough to remove a piece of gravel that had dug its way into the pad of her big toe. She looked around for the first time, truly taking in her surroundings. There was nothing. Nothing but fields, asphalt, and brilliant blue sky. *She was alone. Did anyone ever drive this road? How long could she keep walking, she wondered.*

Certain that Lydia was behind her, she gripped the underside of her belly and pressed on.

Her knees shook, her lungs burned and no matter how much air she inhaled, it wasn't enough to satisfy the burning in her chest. Eventually, her ankle pulsated and gave out. Each time she attempted to bear any weight on it, the pain seared, slicing through her. She had to rely almost solely on one leg. Which made running rather difficult. She could hear the whoosh, whoosh, whoosh of her heartbeat in her ears, and all she could think about was sitting down on the side of that road and calling it a day. *Only she refused to stop altogether. Keep going. Keep going. Keep going... the boys. Think of the boys. And the baby.* When thinking of her family stopped working, and her vision grew fuzzy, she counted. *One, two, three, four...* She went on and on until she forgot which number she was on and then she started all over again.

It wasn't clear how far she'd actually walked when at last she heard the faint familiar hum of a pickup truck. It was distant, but she prayed it was coming her way. *Was she imagining it? No. What if it was Lydia?* As the roar of the engine grew louder, she considered hiding, but she realized she couldn't go on much further. She needed help. She waited as the sound of the motor drew closer. The truck was blue. No, maybe black. That's when she realized that the old pickup truck might not stop and began waving her arms. It slowed. Addison stood there staring and watched as the truck slowed to a full stop. Hesitantly, she met the man's gaze. He was calling out to her.

She couldn't respond. Her voice wouldn't come out no matter how hard she tried to make herself speak.

The man frowned. "Ma'am? Ma'am. Can you hear me? You deaf?"

Addison, her eyes wide, held up the bloody knife.

"Whoa," he said.

Finally, the sound in her throat caught. "Don't come near me," she managed. "I'll cut you."

His eyes shifted downward to her stomach.

"Easy now..." he said putting up his hands.

"Call the police," she ordered.

The man grinned then, flashing his yellow teeth, as a sense of recognition seemed to hit and his whole face lit up. "Say. You're *that* lady, ain't 'cha... There's a woman in town looking for ya. I told her I seen that woman who lives out this way a lot lately, and she kinda looks like that photo they been showing 'round, though, she shorter than you is—I told her I was gone check it out..."

"I said call the police," Addison repeated, her voice barely audible. She thrust the knife into the air once more. The glaring sun overhead reflected against the metal and it was too much for her eyes. She squinted. The truck and its engine were so loud, and nothing made sense.

She covered her ears but kept her gaze on the man.

He considered her for a moment. Filthy, covered in blood, and very pregnant, he must have decided. He straightened up, composed himself, produced a flip phone and then held it out to her. "All right, Miss. I'm callin'," he assured her with a nod. "You just settle down there."

Addison listened as the man spoke to someone on the line. She took three steps backward, until she was nearly in the ditch and then doubled over, giving in to the dry-heaves. Her stomach was too empty to produce any vomit, but this didn't stop the bile from rising and burning her throat.

"You want some water, Miss?" The man called out.

Addison shook her head. *She wasn't taking anything from him.*

"Y'all hurry!" he said into the phone. "She's pukin' her guts up out here. I think she might be dyin'."

Addison gripped the knife feeling the cool, dull edge dig

into her palm. *One, two, three, four...* she started counting again. It could have been minutes or it could have been hours before the police finally showed up. Addison couldn't tell you. She only remembered dropping the knife when the cops rushed toward her, ordering her to put her hands in the air. At first, it all appeared to be happening in slow motion. But then, all of a sudden, everything sped up. The whirlwind of activity and the onslaught of questions took her by surprise. She recalled counting to ten. Then she vaguely remembered seeing her best friend, Jessica, stepping out of a police car and running in her direction.

Everything was happening so fast. It was too much. The lights and the sirens flooded her senses and the screaming, there was so much screaming. She was going under, dying or blacking out, she couldn't be sure which. Her eyes couldn't keep up with the commotion, or the orders being shouted around her. Her ears hurt after so many months of near silence. Her heart was beating too fast. She struggled for breath. She was going to pass out. *One, two, three. Just count. One, two, now breathe.* Her chest tightened.

Being asked to lie back on the stretcher and having an oxygen mask placed on her face was the second to last thing she recalled.

After that, she shut her eyes tight and prayed that she would wake up again. *Please. Please. Please, she whispered. Just breathe.*

Then she let go, at last giving into the exhaustion that overwhelmed her.

～

When Addison awoke next, or at least what she remembered afterward, was being wheeled through the emergency room doors. Everything was so vivid. *If only she could stay focused, maybe her eyes and her brain could coordinate correctly.*

She thought she must have asked after Jessica. "Your friend is here," someone said. "We'll let her back just as soon as we get things situated." The paramedic with kind eyes eventually assured her twice, maybe three times.

Later, as she was being shifted to a more permanent gurney, she screamed out in pain. Someone told her to relax and then added that her husband had arrived. "I need to see him," she pleaded. She panicked, digging her fingers into the sheet.

"You will, very soon," the nurse with the tired gray eyes told her. She patted Addison's arm. "But first, we need you to calm down, okay?"

Addison felt the sting of hot tears as they spilled over and dripped down the sides of her face. "Please," she begged. "Help me."

"You're safe," a voice spoke into her ear. "You're going to be all right." She couldn't see the voice. *Was it Lydia?* The room was spinning. Dizzily, she tried to watch the flurry of activity surrounding her as though it were a movie playing, one where she wasn't the main character. Eventually, when things began to die down, she pled some more and was told they would be bringing William in shortly.

They'd given her a sedative to take the edge off, the gray-eyed nurse informed her. Addison liked her because she got right in her face when she talked. She was firm. She told her the sedative might be why everything seemed strange. Then an older male whom Addison assumed was a doctor asked her several questions. *Her name. The year. The president's name.* He explained briefly that she was in shock and that they were working to stabilize her blood pressure. Whatever else he might have said, she couldn't recall. In the corner, another nurse hung an IV bag. "Why are you doing this?" she screamed, her voice cracking.

"Let's give her a little more morphine," the booming voice ordered.

The nurse turned to her and she could see it wasn't Lydia. She watched the woman press buttons on the monitor above her head. The lights had been dimmed. Her mind raced. She hadn't even thought to ask about the baby. *Had she felt it move recently? She couldn't be sure.*

When she woke again, she felt her husband's presence before she saw him. She studied his face as it grew closer to hers, slowly coming into focus. He looked older than she remembered, tired, and weary.

"Look at you," was all he seemed to be able to get out.

"Look at you," Addison repeated, her voice breaking, her words slurred.

He stood at her side and took her hand in his.

"Don't leave me," she whispered.

He smiled, though just barely, eyed her stomach, and then met her eyes once more. "I'm here," he said, squeezing her hand gently and then he wept.

~

ADDISON DRIFTED. SHE WAS FLOATING ON A MAKESHIFT RAFT somewhere far out. Alarms were going off. The waves were coming in. And they were going out. William shook her gently, and she heard him call out to her. She was there with him, but not really. She watched as the doctors ushered him out of the room.

Her blood pressure was rising, they'd said, and they needed to get it stabilized. She needed further testing.

Banished to the ER waiting room, William sat with his head in his hands until Sondra arrived and spent most of her time trying to keep him calm. He seemed hell-bent on infuriating the staff by asking about his wife approximately every two minutes. He demanded to know when they would be finished accessing her. "How long can these things possibly take?" he kept repeating.

Jess, impatient and annoyed herself, stood and paced before she stopped suddenly. "I was close. *So close...* I mean... I'm still in—I just can't believe we found her. Or that she's pregnant. My God—"

Sondra did a double take and looked to William. "She's pregnant?"

Jess stared at him, his eyes wild. She swallowed. "I didn't have much time to talk with her before the paramedics took over, but she did say it's yours."

His jaw hardened and he cocked his head meeting her gaze head on. "Of course, it's mine."

"I didn't mean it that way," Jess muttered. "I just meant—"

He exhaled loudly. "I don't give a fuck what you meant."

"William," Sondra warned.

Jess sighed. "She's going to be okay..." she said to herself. "She has to be..."

"Where is the bitch who's responsible for this, anyway?" Sondra interjected.

Jess waited for William to answer, and when he didn't, she finally answered. "We don't know. They're searching the property."

$\sim$

ONCE THE DOCTORS HAD FINALLY GOTTEN ADDISON stabilized, they ordered an ultrasound and allowed William back in.

He entered cautiously, which wasn't his style, but the last thing he wanted was to be kicked out again. He searched his wife's face for appropriate words. When nothing came, he simply said, "I'm having the boys flown here."

Addison teared up, but she didn't reply. She was afraid if she did, a dam would break and all the things she held inside would spill out. He took her hand in his.

"I'm scared," she whispered.

"I was, too," he said. "But not anymore."

"Do you want to know the sex?" The sonographer interrupted as she placed the wand on Addison's swollen belly and moved it slowly from side to side.

"No!" They'd both said in unison.

The woman turned back and a 3D image lit up the screen. "That's our baby," William whispered after a few seconds, stroking his wife's forehead.

The sonographer stopped, pressed a button, leaned in, and appeared to study the screen intently. She frowned and then repositioned the screen to face her directly. She placed the wand down, checked Addison's chart, and then picked the wand up once again and placed it to her skin.

"Is everything okay?" Addison asked, her voice quiet.

The sonographer stopped abruptly and removed the wand. She turned the screen to face them, before repositioning the wand. When the image came into focus, she smiled. "Better than okay," she said. "You guys are having two babies."

"Two?" William coughed.

Addison inhaled deeply, her hand instinctively flew to her stomach. "Oh, my God."

The lady narrowed her gaze. "I see that you already have a set of twins."

Addison nodded slightly.

The woman smiled. "Then it makes perfect sense."

William laughed and then leaned down to kiss his wife.

"Yes," he said, shaking his head. "Perfect sense."

BEYOND BEDROCK

CHAPTER TWENTY-SEVEN

The police poured every resource they had into finding Lydia. Dogs were brought in to aid in the search. The last the Hartmans' had heard, they lost her scent two miles into the woods. She had been headed south, that much they knew. William hired bounty hunters. And in the meantime, they tightened their security back at home.

The first letter arrived while Addison was still in the hospital. It was postmarked from a town not far from the Texas/Mexico border.

Dearest William,

I am so very sorry that things did not work out as I had hoped. I wear gray because it is associated with loss and that's what I feel.

But I want you to know that I am fine. I've had my wounds licked and sewn up, and while I'm not completely healed... I am getting there.

At any rate, you should know my love persists. It remains as intact as ever, and I will wait for you.

Also, I hear that we are having twins. Yes, my love. I hear things...

I'm over the moon about the babies and want to tell you that— while I might be gone for now—I understand I am certainly not forgotten.

And for that, I am grateful.

Yours truly,

L

P.S. I wrote you a little something else:

Out of Pocket.

Your love was a currency

I never could afford

Yet I would have given everything—

Emptied out the whole of me.

Just to have a little for myself.

That's the way you wanted it

And I gladly paid the price.

$\approx$

WHEN ADDISON WAS WELL ENOUGH FOR TRAVEL, WILLIAM HAD her transferred back to Austin where doctors kept her for an additional sixteen days. Recovery proved to be a slow process. Her ankle was broken in two places, which required surgery. In addition, she was pretty dehydrated and clearly malnourished. But that was just the physical side of the situation. She worked with a psychologist for hours each day to try to understand how to handle reentry.

The simplest things appeared to be the hardest. Knowing she could go to the bathroom when she wanted—that she didn't have to hold it for fear of the stench. Having electricity and hot and cold food again, it all took some getting used to. Any new faces, any change in her surroundings, was enough to make her freeze up and panic. Everything seemed new. Everything seemed different.

William, for the most part, refused to leave the hospital. Jess sat with Addison whenever William wasn't—the two of them taking turns so that one of them was always present. William always took the night shift. On this particular day, like many of the others, Jess watched Addison sleep. She checked the time on her computer, and after realizing that William was due back any moment, she closed the laptop and shoved it in her bag. As she stood to stretch, her friend stirred.

"Hey," Addison whispered, startling her.

Jess turned. "Hey, there…" she said. "I didn't want to wake you. They said you had a rough night…"

Addison eyed her friend as though she were trying to grasp something that was just out of reach.

Jess waited for her to respond and when she didn't she moved in closer. "Can I get you anything?"

"Sit down," Addison urged.

Jessica looked surprised, but she did as she was told.

Addison propped herself up on her elbows and pulled herself to a seated position. "I had a dream…"

"Oh, yeah?" Jess said, but she didn't pry. Addison had yet to talk about anything in terms of what had happened to her, and Jess wasn't one to push. She knew Addison, and she knew that she would talk when she was ready.

It appeared that time had come.

Addison took a deep breath, held it in, and then released it. She spoke slowly, carefully. "Bryan was my friend," she said. "For months, Jess, he was my only friend." She paused to look up at the ceiling. "He was just a boy… you know." Jess shifted then. Addison's eyes had filled with tears.

Jess reached for the box of tissue on the nightstand and placed them in Addison's lap. She didn't tell her it was okay to cry. She showed her.

"I want to talk about it… but I can't."

Jessica pursed her lips. "You can't?"

"The thing is, Jess… it's hard to explain. I'm not sure there's anyone in the world who could possibly understand," she said, brushing the tears from her cheeks. "Bryan understood."

"I can try," Jess replied. "I want to try…"

Addison deadpanned. "But you cannot know what it is like to survive that kind of situation until you've been in it. The first time, when I was kidnapped by Scott Hammons, it was for a couple of days, and I'm not sure why… but it didn't seem to have as profound of an effect on me as it did this time. I'm not the same person I was before. And yet, it's as though everyone expects me to be what I was. I'm not her. Six months in captivity changes a person… "

"I'm sure," Jess said.

"It's the mind games, the not knowing that really did me in. In that cabin, *everything* was life and death. Everything, Jess. Out here, it all just seems trivial. Things like shopping lists, and parties, and vacations… you know, petty things like who said what and who doesn't like who. Pretty much everything that makes up small talk… none of these things matter anymore—and my biggest fear is that my life will never feel normal again."

"Whose life *is* normal, Addison?" Jess asked with a shrug. "Take a look at the people around you. Is my life normal? No. Is your husband's life normal? Certainly not. Normal, whatever that is, is overrated."

"Maybe. But an entire six months of my life are just… gone. Everyone went on living their lives and mine consisted of one tiny room. For six months, I stared at the same four plywood walls."

"I've read the letters you wrote," Jess said. "And you're right, I can't understand, but I can imagine—"

Addison swallowed hard.

"Has William read them?" Jess asked.

"Yes."

"And how are things with you two?"

"He's angry. And he seems to be managing it in his normal 'I can handle it all' elusive way, but also, he's changed, too. He has taken steps in the right direction and honestly, the rest of it, the reason I went to the beach house... it all seems pretty... irrelevant. I realize that probably doesn't make any sense—and sure, there are things we need to work out... but the thing is, when the bullshit falls away, and you see life for what it is—short—and fleeting—and really fucking scary—well, it just makes who you spend it with all that much more important."

Jessica nodded. She didn't speak for several minutes. When she did, she spit it out, all at once. "Tell me about Bryan, Addison."

Addison flinched at the sound of his name. She started to speak and then hesitated before she finally exhaled and let it out. "Okay... Well... I guess... I'm not even sure where to start, so— I'll go with this... The thing that one misses the most when being held captive is touch. That's what I missed the most outside of the normal stuff like you guys and pizza." She smiled and then she went on. "Sometimes, I would hold Bryan's hand, and we would sit quietly like that for hours. Just holding hands. It was so simple and yet so significant, you know? Sometimes I would scoot over to him, he would lay his head in my lap, and I would stroke his hair. He told me no one had ever done that to him before. It wasn't anything romantic—not even remotely. It was simply two friends who understood one another without the need for words. And it's funny, because, the more time we spent together, and the more we got to know one another, the more I realized Bryan was really smart, actually. He'd had a tough life and he'd gotten into some trouble... a friend had asked him to pick up some tools for him, which he agreed to do only to find out they were stolen after he was caught in possession of them. Not long after that, he told me he took a date swimming on private property and got busted, and because he had just gotten out of trouble and was on probation for it, the trespassing turned out to be a bigger offense, and he served nine days in jail. After that, he had a hard time getting any sort of job and without family to help him, he was on his own. That's how he ended up down south working at the hardware store in the town where his uncle lived. He didn't have a car and had been sleeping in a tent on his uncle's property. He told me that it was his third day at the hardware store when Lydia pulled up and rolled her window down, and the truth was, he really needed the forty bucks, or he wouldn't have had much to eat until he got his first paycheck. Also, he wanted to give his uncle a few bucks for gas for the rides he'd been giving him, and he thought it would be nice not to have to rely on him for a ride that night. The worst part was, he said he never even thought Lydia might be lying until he noticed the padlocks on the bedroom door, and by that time, well, as you know… it was already too late."

"I'm sorry," Jess said.

"Me, too. Bryan was the first to feel the baby move outside of me. He was my friend, and it's my fault he's dead. He died for my freedom."

"It's not your fault, Addison."

"He's dead, isn't he? And here I am. Alive."

"But you didn't kill him."

Addison rolled over and closed her eyes. "It was my plan, Jess. I came up with it. And I knew the chances were slim to none that it would work. So—I don't know. I just couldn't watch him suffer anymore. It was selfish. So… if I'm not at fault, then who is…"

"Lydia."

"But I lied to him, Jess. I told him it would work. It didn't. I told him we would be free. When the truth was, only one of us would. And that's the thing, you know… the best liars always stick close to the truth."

~

WILLIAM LOADED THE LAST OF ADDISON'S THINGS ONTO THE cart. They were finally headed home, which was a good thing because the walls were beginning to close in. Addison couldn't take one more night in that hospital. William had arranged for her to have care at home, and once she learned she was being discharged the following morning, she'd finally gotten a decent night's sleep, at least one without as many nightmares.

Addison shuffled through the stack of get-well cards that Sondra had left on the nightstand. She cleared her throat. "I don't think I'm going back to work…"

William turned and jutted his bottom lip out. "No?"

"I don't know. It just seems so far off. I try, but I can't imagine that kind of normalcy at this point."

He narrowed his gaze. "What made you think about work?"

She shrugged. "I don't know what I'm going to do to fill the time now. What if I go crazy?"

William raised his brow. "I have a feeling you'll have your hands full soon enough."

"Yeah…"

"We need to start thinking about the babies' nursery, don't you think…"

Addison pressed her hands into the curve of her back. "Probably."

"Do you want me to handle it?"

"No," she said. "I'll get Jess to take care of it. She's good at that sort of stuff."

He raised his eyebrows. "You don't want to do it?"

Addison turned to face him full on. "I hadn't really thought about it… I guess you could say that I've been sort of preoccupied."

William sat on the edge of the hospital bed, reached for her hand, and when she placed it in his, he pulled his wife to him. He started to place his hands on her belly but stopped. "Is this okay?" She nodded. He took her face in his hands. "I know you're angry. I get it. I know what it feels like to be scared to have someone touch you. But you haven't really talked to me about any of it."

She swallowed and then softened. "I'm not sure I can."

"I realize it may not feel like it, but we're in this together," he said. "And… I just want you to know that I'm here if you want to talk. But I also understand if you don't."

"Tell me what it was like… with your stepfather."

William swallowed. "About like you can imagine, I'm sure."

She could and she didn't want to. She let it go. *Maybe everything didn't need to be said.* "Is therapy helping?" she finally asked.

"It is and it isn't."

Addison bit her lip. "What do you mean?"

"I don't know." He shrugged. "It's just… sometimes, it feels okay to talk about, and sometimes, it's the last thing I want to do."

"So what do you do?"

"We talk about other things. Normal stuff…"

"You hate it, don't you?"

His jaw tightened. "I understand therapy, and I understand that it's a necessary evil on occasion, but I also think there are other ways of handling things."

"Is that why you didn't tell me about Sondra?"

"No. I didn't tell you about Sondra because I was ashamed."

She sighed and looked away. "I don't think I got that before. I was so angry. I wanted to be enough for you. And to think that I wasn't...well—"

"You are enough. You were always enough—"

Addison placed her finger to his lips, silencing him. "I get it now... you had needs that I wasn't meeting. I can be pissed about it, or I can deal with reality. And the truth is, if I had dealt with reality, I would've seen that... before."

"It doesn't make lying okay, though. Relationships are hard to maintain, even with complete honesty. Especially with complete honesty. But what I've learned is... once you start lying about who you are and what you need... it becomes damned near impossible to make it work. Everyone gives themselves away somehow..."

"Then let's not lie."

He smiled. "I'm with you on that."

"I'd prefer to do the not lying, this is who I am, take it or leave it sort of thing..."

He raised his brow and placed his hands on the curve of her hips. "I like it."

She smiled. "I've always liked it."

"That a girl."

She laughed then, though just barely. *That always was the best sound, he thought.* "Have you seen me lately?" she asked gesturing toward her swollen belly.

"I have. And you're more beautiful than I've ever seen."

Addison rolled her eyes. "Right. Have you seen these scars?" She pointed at her ankle.

"Have you seen mine?"

She met his gaze directly.

William stroked her face with the back of his hand "Scars

make a person interesting, Addison. Now—we just match better, that's all."

"I keep seeing her face. And it's my face. That's the fucked up part."

He pursed his lips. "We're going to find her."

"Yeah, well," she choked. "I'm not so sure…"

"You don't have to be."

Addison frowned.

He stood. "I'm sure enough for the both of us."

❧

EPILOGUE

Addison Hartman was at home for approximately twenty-two hours before she was rushed back to the hospital with preterm labor. Two days after that, she gave birth to twin girls, Charlotte and Isabelle, with William at her side.

The girls were tiny, weighing in at three and three and a half pounds each. But they were healthy and their parents were over the moon.

The moment that tiny bundle was placed in his arms, William Hartman knew he was a changed man. Nothing else in the world would ever matter as much as this did.

He wasn't sure, as he nervously stroked Addison's head while the doctors cut her open. He kept asking if she was okay. But just as she'd expected, the second he first heard that faint cry, all attention shifted to his child. "What was it? Was she okay? How much did she weigh? What was her Apgar score?"

Addison knew exactly the kind of father her husband would be. It was exactly the kind of man and husband he was. Overwhelming, controlling, infuriating, and yet, more loving and more present than anyone she'd ever met.

When the nurse placed 'Baby A' in his arms, he froze. Addison watched his face. *Nothing would ever be the same.* "She's so… little…" he whispered.

Addison strained to try to catch a peek, but the sedative was taking its toll. While she was no stranger to having a caesarean, they'd given her extra sedative due to the PTSD she suffered. She foresaw being tied down would be a trigger and realized that now not even the happiest moment would be normal for her. *Nothing would ever be the same.*

Lydia and Scott Hammons had stolen so much from her, but she refused them this.

She willed herself to smile, she willed herself to stay present. This time, when she counted, it meant something. *Two girls. Not one. But two.*

"Can you believe it?" William asked as he held up their daughter.

She smiled and studied the tiny face. "No," she said.

"She looks just like you."

Addison blinked back tears. She felt another tug followed by an angry cry. 'Baby B' was out.

William handed the baby off to a nurse as a second nurse placed 'Baby B' in his arms.

His face beamed. "Wow. This one, too…"

Addison watched as he stared at their daughter. "I can't believe it—" he started. The nurse interrupted. "We need to get little sister under some oxygen."

William nodded and then carefully, and somewhat hesitantly, handed the baby over. He turned to his wife.

"How did we get so lucky?" he asked.

She swallowed. "I have no idea."

～

THREE DAYS LATER, THE FOUR OF THEM WERE RELEASED FROM the hospital. Once again, it had been arranged for Addison and the babies to receive care at home. Everything down to the most minute detail had been planned out, coordinated and arranged.

It had apparently become William's life's work to see that all was taken care of and was running smoothly. All staff was carefully monitored and checked, and the level of security they possessed was unprecedented. He liked to remind Addison of this time and time again.

The boys were thrilled with the new arrivals, and Addison, admittedly this go around, found that having twins were vastly different when one had this much help. Jessica had practically moved in, and Addison's primary focus was reconnecting with her sons. She understood that the babies didn't need her as much as her older children. They wouldn't know the difference. Besides, their father was enamored with them anyway. If Addison ever wanted to know where the girls were, the response was most often in William's arms.

It was a blissfully exhausting, happy time.

～

UNTIL EIGHT DAYS AFTER THEIR HOMECOMING, WHEN ANOTHER letter arrived. This one postmarked from Monterey, Mexico.

Dearest William,

Congratulations on the birth of our babies!
I cannot wait to meet Isabelle and Charlotte.
It's only a matter of time and we will be together.

That said, so far, I have managed to blend in well here. I'm a girl who knows how *not* to be seen. I've done it my whole life.

My long hair is gone, and I now wear it short.

And I have good news of my own!

I've met someone. A couple. I'll call them Shawn and Eleanor (for now) and they are American.

Eleanor is an odd broad. She is what they call a cuckquean. Which I learned basically just means she likes to pick up women and watch them sleep with her husband. It's really interesting and totally my thing… because, you know, I like to watch people suffer. And, boy, does she suffer as she watches the two of us. Lucky me though, it turns out that the bastard is actually a pretty amazing lover. He's a sick bastard—nothing at all like you, but he sure knows how to fuck a woman into the next city—if you know what I mean.

Shawn (obviously not his real name) is currently hanging in a secret undisclosed location. I've sent his crazy wife on a little scavenger hunt. If she wants her husband back, she's going to have to learn a little lesson.

And I tell you what… this is really quite a fun game we're playing here, William.

Until we are together again, I will sharpen my skills. I know you appreciate that sort of thing.

Give Addison my best.

And kiss the babies for me.

See you soon.

Yours truly,

L

P.S. More poetry. For you:

From The Inside Out.

I wanted to tell you everything.

More than you knew

But I couldn't…

So I ate the words—

too raw to speak.

Only the joke was on me.

Who knew?

They would eat me alive,

from the inside out.

∼

WILLIAM SENT A TEAM DOWN TO MEXICO WHERE THEY SPENT three weeks searching for Lydia Hammons. It was a search that ultimately proved futile. The following week, another letter arrived. This one postmarked Cancun, Mexico.

Dearest William,

The scavenger hunt got boring, and the kitty killed her mice if you catch my drift.

I've headed further south.

You know what's great here? Tourists. Silly, drunken tourists. Recently, I met a couple celebrating their tenth anniversary. And do you have any idea what they wanted to celebrate with? A threesome. Not my kind of gift. But what can you do? People these days, I swear! They're all so immoral.

You'll be happy to know that I obliged their little fantasy.

And then I showed them mine. I starved them like the little rats they are. They were filth, William. And I took out the trash.

But aside from that, I have news!

I've decided that the time spent apart from one another shouldn't be in vain. I want to make you proud, William.

I want our time away from one another to mean something.

So! I've decided on a new career path. You've inspired me! I'm going to write about and publish my travels and little escapades I find along the way. I'm going to detail it all. In a book! I know! Right? I'm sure you can't believe it. I can hardly process it all myself. I'm going to be an author! I'll have a nom de plume, of course. But how great would it be to have you as my first reader. This way, we can always stay close in our time apart.

I hope it won't be too long.

In fact, I know it won't.

Look for something soon.

Oh, William. I miss you. Kiss those babies for me and know that our little family will be reunited before you know it.

First, I just need to take out a few immoral evildoers. They have no place in this world with our children.

Yours truly,

L

P.S. I wrote you another poem:

Dreams To Come.

I dreamt of you last night.

Which is nothing new.

It happens from time to time.

Still, I hate the way you so easily creep into my dreams.

The way you waltz right on into my mind—

like you own the place.

And occupy every corner.

Though I let you...

Because that's what love does.

ADDISON SAT CROSS-LEGGED ON THE FLOOR AND STARED AT her husband. "The babies are six months old now... and I was thinking..."

He raised his brow. "Oh?"

"Yeah..."

"Addison, don't play with me."

She smiled. "I think we should take a trip..."

William cocked his head to the side. "Where to?"

"Mexico."

He deadpanned. "Absolutely not."

"We have to find her, William. Before she finds us. Otherwise, it'll always be this way… us here just waiting."

"We're not waiting."

She scoffed. "Aren't we, though?"

"I said no, Addison. Leave it alone."

"She almost killed me, William. She almost killed our children."

"Yeah, and that's a pretty good reason not to go looking for her, don't you think…"

"She'll always be looking for us is what I think. I'd certainly rather be the hunter than the hunted."

William stood and went to her. He reached out his hand and pulled her off the floor, taking her in his arms. "Please. Stop. We have a family. There's risk and then there's stupidity. I do agree we need to take a trip. Maybe even solo. But not to Mexico."

She pulled back. "I don't feel safe with her out there. I don't think I can live my life this way, William."

He searched her face. "What are you saying?"

"I'm saying I feel like a prisoner in my own home."

"We'll move."

"Where? I can't just uproot the boys. They have school and friends and…"

"Okay," he said, looking away. "Give me three months," he added, meeting her eye. "That's all I'm asking for is three months…"

She shook her head. "She's out there doing to others what she did to us. Three months and more people die."

"I am not putting you at risk, Addison. So we find her. Then what?"

"I don't know. We kill her."

"Addison, do you even hear what you're saying?"

"Yes, and I know it sounds crazy, but I can't just sit here and do nothing while she—"

"Maybe it's time for you to go back to work."

"Maybe it is," she said, rearing back. "Actually— I've given it some thought…"

He cocked his head to the side. "Really?"

"Yeah. And I'm considering starting a company that focuses on finding missing persons."

William raised his brow. "That sounds like an excellent idea."

She grinned and then let it slowly fade. "It is," she said. "And I'm going to start with Lydia Hammons."

~

ADDISON DID START WITH LYDIA HAMMONS, AND SHE AND William did end up going down to Mexico, but just once, three months later, true to his word. Unfortunately, for the two of them, they did not locate Lydia. But they were able to locate three of her victims' bodies and bring them home to their respective families using the information she provided in her letters.

Lydia Hammons is wanted for murder in three countries.

Addison and William Hartman and their family have since moved to an undisclosed location.

Lydia's letters still continue to show up at their former address. She writes that she is penning her first book, a memoir. Addison only hopes that it will bring her closer to finding Lydia Hammons and holding her responsible for the crimes she has committed.

The twins are fourteen months old, and today, they play underneath the shade of an old oak tree on their property. This is where Uncle Bryan's remains are buried, their mother tells them, although they are too young to understand.

She watches them toddle along and the phone rings,

which brings news of another couple gone missing while on vacation. It is not surprising, but this is what keeps her going.

She jots down the details and texts them to her husband.

He texts back that he loves her. Because he knows it's what she needs to hear.

She tells him she's counting the minutes until he gets home. Because she is.

Later, after dinner, after they've made love, they'll do what they do most nights and discuss their latest findings.

This is their normal now. And it's okay. It is better than okay. It is beautiful.

They work together and it brings them one step closer to a day when they'll finally have closure.

Until that day, they press on.

～

A NOTE FROM BRITNEY

Dear Reader,

I hope you enjoyed reading *Beyond Bedrock*. If you have a moment and you'd like to let me know what you thought, feel free to drop me an email (britney@britneyking.com).

Writing a book is an interesting adventure, but letting other people read it is like inviting them into your brain to rummage around. *This is what I like. This is the way I think.*

That feeling can be intense and interesting.

Thank you, again for reading my work. I don't have the backing or the advertising dollars of big publishing, but hopefully I have something better... readers who like the same kind of stories I do. If you are one of them please share with your friends and consider helping out by doing one (or all) of these quick things:

1. Drop me an email and let me know what you thought.

britney@britneyking.com

2. Visit my Review Page and write a 30 second review (even short ones make a big difference).

http://britneyking.com/aint-too-proud-to-beg-for-reviews/

Many readers don't realize what a difference reviews make but they make ALL the difference.

3. If you'd like to make sure you don't miss anything, to receive an email whenever I release a new title, sign up for my new release newsletter at:

https://britneyking.com/new-release-alerts/

Thanks for helping, and for reading *Beyond Bedrock*. It means a lot. Be sure to check out the second book in my latest series, *Water Under The Bridge* at the end of this book, as well as via your favorite retailer.

Britney King

Austin, Texas

December 2017

ABOUT THE AUTHOR

Britney King lives in Austin, Texas with her husband, children, two dogs, one ridiculous cat, and a partridge in a peach tree.

When she's not wrangling the things mentioned above, she writes psychological, domestic and romantic thrillers set in suburbia.

Without a doubt, she thinks connecting with readers is the best part of this gig. You can find Britney online here:

Email: britney@britneyking.com
Web: https://britneyking.com
Facebook: https://www.facebook.com/BritneyKingAuthor
Instagram: https://www.instagram.com/britneyking_/
Twitter: https://twitter.com/BritneyKing_
Goodreads: https://bit.ly/BritneyKingGoodreads
Pinterest: https://www.pinterest.com/britneyking_/

Happy reading.

ACKNOWLEDGMENTS

First, thank YOU. Yep, I mean *you*, dear reader. Because I like people who like books—and because obviously, if you picked this one up, you have good taste. I also (surprise!) happen to like people with good taste. ;)

Many thanks to Sebastian Kullas for providing the perfect cover image.

To my friends in the book world—you guys are the icing on the cake. From fellow authors to the amazing bloggers who put so much effort forth simply for the love of sharing books. To my people in PR to the beta readers to my street team and strongest supporters. Naming each of you would be a novel in and of itself—but I trust that you know who you are and I want to thank you. Times infinity.

A special thanks to my very first readers, you know who you are.

Again—because it deserves to be said twice, I'd like to thank the readers. For every kind word, for simply reading... you guys are the best. I could be making this up... but studies show that nine out of ten readers are good people. Thank you for being that.

madman hell-bent on revenge. The series has been compared to Fatal Attraction, Single White Female, and Basic Instinct.

Around The Bend

Around The Bend, is a heart-pounding standalone which traces the journey of a well-to-do suburban housewife, and her life as it unravels, thanks to the secrets she keeps. If she were the only one with things she wanted to keep hidden, then maybe it wouldn't have turned out so bad. But she wasn't.

Somewhere With You | Book One
Anywhere With You | Book Two
The With You Series Box Set

The With You Series at its core is a deep love story about unlikely friends who travel the world; trying to find themselves, together and apart. Packed with drama and adventure along with a heavy dose of suspense, it has been compared to The Secret Life of Walter Mitty and Love, Rosie.

In the tradition of *Gone Girl* and *Behind Closed Doors* comes a gripping, twisting, furiously clever read that demands your attention, and keeps you guessing until the very end. For fans of the anti-heroine and stories told in unorthodox ways, *Water Under The Bridge* delivers us the perfect dark and provocative villain.

As a woman who feels her clock ticking every single moment of the day, former bad girl Kate Anderson is desperate to reinvent herself. So when she sees a handsome stranger walking toward her, she feels it in her bones, there's no time like the present. *He's the one.*

Kate vows to do whatever it takes to have what she wants, even if that something is becoming someone else. Now, ten pounds thinner, armed with a new name, and a plan, she's this close to living the perfect life she's created in her mind.

But Kate has secrets.

And too bad for her, that handsome stranger has a few of his own.

With twists and turns you won't see coming, Water Under The Bridge examines the pressure that many women feel to "have it all" and introduces a protagonist whose hard edges and cutthroat ambition will leave you questioning your judgment and straddling the line between what's right and wrong.

Enjoy dark fiction? Are you a fan of stories told in unique ways? If so, you'll love Britney King's bestselling psychological thrillers. Get to know Jude and Kate, unreliable narrators at best, intense, and, in your face at worst. *Water Under The Bridge* is the first book in The Water Trilogy. Available in digital and print.

DEAD IN THE WATER (Book Two) and *COME HELL OR HIGH WATER* (Book Three) are now available.

What readers are saying:

"Another amazingly well-written novel by Britney King. It's every bit as dark, twisted and mind twisting as Water Under The Bridge...maybe even a little more so."

"Hands down- best book by Britney King. Yet. She has delivered a difficult writing style so perfectly and effortlessly, that you just want to worship the book for the writing. The author has managed to make murder/assassination/accidental- gunshot-to-the-head- look easy. Necessary."

"Having fallen completely head over heels for these characters and this author with the first book in the series, I've been pretty much salivating over the thought of this book for months now. You'll be glad to know that it did not disappoint!"

Series Praise

"If Tarantino were a woman and wrote novels... they might read a bit like this."

"Fans of Gillian Flynn and Paula Hawkins meet your next obsession."

"Provocative and scary."

"A dark and edgy page-turner. What every good thriller is made of."

"I devoured this novel in a single sitting, absolutely enthralled by the storyline. The suspense was clever and unrelenting!"

"Completely original and complex."

"Compulsive and fun."

"No-holds-barred villains. Fine storytelling full of mystery and suspense."

"Fresh and breathtaking insight into the darkest corners of the human psyche."

WATER UNDER THE BRIDGE

BRITNEY KING

COPYRIGHT

Hot Banana Press

Cover Design by Britney King LLC

Cover Image by Grant Reid Photography

Copy Editing by Librum Artis Editorial Services &

RMJ Manuscript Services

Proofread by Proofreading by the Page

First Edition: 2016

ISBN: 978-0-9966497-2-8 (Paperback)

ISBN: 978-0-9966497-4-2 (All E-Books)

britneyking.com

For the Lovers—
for there are few things as easy or as hard as loving.

PREFACE

There's a girl long dead who rests down by the water's edge.
Her final words were, "No. Don't. Please. I'm sorr—."
She never did get the second half of her apology out.
I made sure she never will.
Some things are best left unsaid, I think.
In the end, it didn't matter.
I knew she was sorry.
And she knew it too.

~

There's a girl who rests down by the water's edge.
She was beautiful, but you and the water washed it all away.
You think I don't know what you've done, but I do.
I know that you visit on occasion, and I know other
things too.

~

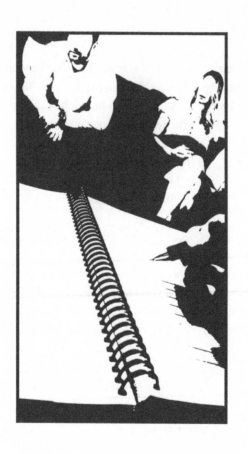

CHAPTER ONE

JUDE

AFTER

Your face crumbles as the judge hands down our sentence. I am fascinated by the way your expression changes, as slowly, recognition takes over that unlike the rest of your affairs, this one isn't going to be a one-and-done deal. Turns out, lucky us, the great State of Texas is having a go at a pilot program designed to drop the state's divorce rate.

But you aren't feeling very lucky. Not at all. I can tell by the way you pinch the bridge of your nose. You've always hated not getting your way. It doesn't matter anyway. I want to tell you—whatever political agenda bullshit this latest program entails—I can assure you and the rest of Texas, it won't save us. Even if I were the kind of man who believed in miracles, you and me, we'd need a miracle plus a Hail Mary. You've said it yourself, where we are concerned, there is no hope. And this is why you plead.

"Excuse me, your Honor—," you start, and you pause for effect, always the performer. "This really isn't necessary," you profess and then you swallow, and I like it when you're unsure. You go on. "My hus—Jude and I—," you tell him, and you look over at me, and my god, Kate, you've always done indifference so well. "I think we can both agree we're ready to get on with our lives."

You refer to me as your husband—or almost, anyway—and for a moment, I recall what it felt like before your words were laced with poison, back when there was nothing but hope.

I listen to you say your piece, and this time is no different than all the times before, only this time, we have witnesses, and you know how I've always hated that. You must know this because you sink back in your chair, proud.

Your pride doesn't last long because when the judge lists out the terms of our captivity, you glare at your attorney, willing her to save you, but she won't—she can't. You almost choke when he orders six months of marriage counseling, which includes weekly appointments. Your hand flies to your throat, and I remember what that's like, holding you in place, having it all in the palm of my hand. I'd give anything—maybe even your life—to know what that feels like again.

The good news here is the judge and I seem to be on the same page as he informs the two of us that a therapist of our choosing must sign off before the court will grant our divorce. You hold your breath as he speaks, and I remember what that felt like too.

I try, for you, though... I do. I wait for him to finish, and then I tell him that you're right, we've made our decision, and as I speak, you sulk, but isn't this what you've always wanted, to be right? It's hard to look at you, sulking or other-wise, and it never used to be this way.

You're tanner than the last time I saw you. But then, I guess time away did you good. You said you needed your space, and I let you have it. But you have to know, Kate, it was hard not to follow. Maybe I should have. But it was all the same to you—you made up your mind, and your decision settled mine.

Nevertheless, if there is such a thing as a clean break for you and me, it isn't looking good, and it certainly won't be handed down today. This judge does not cease his interminable vendetta against your freedom. He does not relent. You aren't happy, and I can't recall the last time you were, even though I try. It'll come to me, the memory of you, but this courtroom is too stuffy, and you know how I've always hated an audience.

The judge looks away, and you look on, defeated; it's clear, even if you refuse to let it show. As he jots something down, you bite your lip, a tell—you still believe there's hope. But I know better. When he looks up, holding a pen and our future in his hands, you tell him you'd be better off dead, and he looks surprised, as though he's missed something. He has. A lot of somethings. He asks if there's a history of violence. No, you tell him, it was just an expression. Although a part of me wonders if you're right about that too. Maybe there's truth in what you say. Maybe you would be better off dead, and I can't help but wonder if I have it in me.

∽

You text, and there's something about seeing your name light up my phone that still gets me even after all this time. You're all business with your words, and I remember how much I've always liked this side of you. You write that our first therapy session is on Tuesday, and it's so like you to take control, so like you to try and set the pace. But you are mistaken, Kate. Our first therapy session is Monday, and you seem to forget that I'm always one step ahead. You cease with the texting and ring me instead because you like to be the one calling the shots. You're ready to pounce when I offer formalities I don't mean—meanwhile, I'm just happy to hear your voice. You sound exasperated, and I wish I could see your face. No one tells you how much you can miss a person's face. You rattle off instructions, but we don't talk about things, not really, and I wonder when we stopped talking.

We're talking now, that's what you'd say. But I won't—because no one's really saying anything. Nothing worth saying, anyway. Eventually, after I've refused to take the bait because I won't give you my anger as freely as you give yours, you relent, and you agree to the Monday appointment. You'd never admit it, but you like it when I put you in your place. Better to get it over with, you tell me with an edge. The sooner to see you, my dear, I think. But I don't say this. I give you what you want. I always have.

~

You sit cross-legged with your hands folded neatly in your lap, and I hate how pretty you look. Your hair is up, neat and orderly, different, and I study that spot on your neck, the one I know so well. It's your weak spot, and given the chance, I'd dive right in. But we're here, not there, in more ways than one, and I hate that this middle-aged doctor is checking you out. I don't know why you had to wear such a low-cut top, and I recognize the look he gives you. He has a weakness too. But he thinks he's the one in charge here—I can tell by the way he wears it via the chip on his shoulder—when, in reality, he lacks a real MD behind his name. He'd better watch himself. I'll kill him if I have to. He isn't old, the way I'd imagined, and I silently curse myself for not doing more research on something so important.

"Dr. C." That's how he introduces himself, and it's clear he's the kind of fellow who believes in make-believe. What a joke this is—what a joke he is. We would laugh about this, you and I, if things were different. If now were before. But it isn't, and no one's laughing.

"So...why don't you tell me where things went wrong...?" he urges, and I want to hate him, and I almost do, but I admire his directness. I, too, am eager to get to the point.

You shrug, and then I do the same because I'm well-versed in the art of mirroring, but mostly because I want to know your answer. I'm glad he starts here because he doesn't know us, Kate, this fake doctor. He doesn't know that other doctors (both real and fake) have told us we're not capable of love. But we were capable, you and I. We were. We weren't make-believe like this guy. We didn't pretend we were something we weren't until we did—and that is the real reason we're here, but I don't say this. I let you lead the way.

"Is there really any way to know, Doc—" you start and then you stop. You don't call him 'doctor,' but you let him think he's in charge, and I like that you're on to him, too. You know his ability to ask a good question doesn't make him a real doctor, and this is a good start. Already, we're getting somewhere, you and I, and I'm starting to feel something that looks a lot like hope.

You are right, I tell him. There's really no way of knowing where things went bad, no way to pinpoint exactly who's at fault, and yet here we are, sitting in these chairs, talking to him instead of each other, both wanting nothing more than to be anywhere else, getting on with our lives.

You nod, and we're on the same page again, and all of a sudden the world seems less bleak.

He asks how we met, and you crinkle your nose.

"Does it really matter?" I ask. "It's over," I say. "Isn't it best to let it be?" I add for good measure, showing that I, too, can ask good questions. You sit up a little straighter, but you drop your guard.

"Perhaps," he says, even though he and I both know he

doesn't mean it. *Perhaps.* Give me a break. He doesn't know how much I hate that word, but you do, and I see the corners of your lips turn upward as he says it. It doesn't matter, though. He isn't fooling me with his half-hearted response. 'Dr. C' is a man used to being right. He likes control, he likes being in charge, he gets off on toying with people's emotions, and perhaps I could show him the error of his ways.

"And yet—," he adds, as though he's exasperated when he hardly knows what it means to lift a finger, "I want to go back to where it began." He speaks to me as he looks at you, and I can't blame him. They say living well is the best form of revenge. They are right, and in this case, it's pretty apparent —I am bad at revenge.

"I think it would be a good idea for the two of you to tell each other the story of your coming together—in writing," he says, looking from you to me and back, and I can't be mad at him for staring at your tits when he has such good ideas. "I find writing helps clients come to terms with the dissolution of their marriage in a way that merely talking doesn't…" he continues, pausing for added effect, and you cross your arms. "Writing can be reflective. I find it helps my clients to move on, and more importantly, it lends to healthier relationships in the future."

"I don't write," you tell him, as you shift in your seat—you little liar, you. You write all the time.

"You wrote the text you sent me about this very appointment," I say because he needs to know those tits he's staring at are *my* tits and that we still talk. You give me that look, the one I know so well, and perhaps you are onto me.

"Just give it a try," the fake doctor insists, adjusting his glasses on his nose, and I'd pay money to prove they aren't even prescription. "Trust me," he says, and I don't. I hope you don't either. "It'll save the two of you time talking to me," he adds. It's a small offer of condolence, and thankfully, he says something I like. Only this guy doesn't know you like I do. He may have me convinced, but he hasn't convinced you, and you are not soothed. I can tell by the way you check your phone every two and a half seconds. You're distracted, and you don't trust him. You don't want to talk to him, and I hate that phone for getting more of you than you give to us.

"What happens if I just don't come back?" you ask, and this isn't a threat—you genuinely want to know. You, always the stubborn one, always the one to test the limits, until suddenly, you just don't.

"Well—" he says, and I can tell you've tested him. He's intrigued by your defiance, and I will squash him if he gets any ideas...just like I will squash that phone of yours if you don't stop staring at it. "It's mandatory if you want to wrap up your divorce," he tells you, and I like the direction he's going. I like that he plays hardball, so I don't have to. "Furthermore, you'd be violating a court order, and of course, that's not something I'd advise."

You look over at me, and I smile, and you are so clever. You're not the kind of girl who enjoys being backed against the wall—until you are, and that's exactly what I'm imagining doing right now. I think he is too, and perhaps I'll let it slide, but only because I can tell by your expression you understand he's forcing you to come back here, back to me.

"Fine," you say, and it's too bad you're not a mind reader.

"I'll give it a try," you tell him, and you sigh. You check your phone again, and this is a new one, but then, you've always surprised me with your intelligence. You look up, only this time not at me, and I get that familiar pain in my chest I know all to well. "Now, can I go?" you ask, raising your brow, and you're ready to pounce if the answer that comes isn't the one you want.

"Yes," he says, and you stand. You're about to bolt when he stops you with the flick of a wrist, and I remember when I could do that. "That is—if you agree, Jude. I need a commitment here that you'll both come prepared with something in hand by our next appointment," he adds, and there's authority in his voice when he speaks. You wait, and you listen, and this isn't the girl I know. He's looking at me now as though he and I are on the same team. We aren't, and he can't know how much you both love and hate authority, and maybe this is the answer to his question about where it all went wrong.

"Sure," I tell him, offering my best smile. "I'll come up with something for you, Doc," I offer as though I'm his star student, when in fact, I'm full of shit. But he buys it, and you are antsy because you know I've won. "I'll write you a whole book, if that's what it takes," I add for good measure. He smiles. "I'll call it Water Under the Bridge," I say, fucking with you. You shake your head at me. Then you roll your eyes and start for the door. I'm pretty sure you know he's checking out your ass, and he'd better watch himself. There was a time when this wouldn't have bothered me, a time when I believed in you... when I believed in us.

Now is not that time.

~

Learn more at: britneyking.com